County Lines

By

Scott McGowan

for

Kim and Deborah

One Foot in the Grave

Liam awoke with a start. His vision was blurred, his eyes cloying with sleep but he was just able to make out the off-white vision of a ceiling he did not recognise. When his senses began to return, he realised that he was lying, flat-out and naked on a cold, *cold* table.

Allowing panic to overtake him, Liam rolled off of the table. His legs collapsed under him; his throat setting free an involuntary shriek as he folded onto the stone floor. It was only due to base instinct that he managed to drag himself towards the edge of the room. Every movement was like a lesson in pain. He only stopped when he was able to slump down with his back against the wall and observe his surroundings.

He sat there, his breath visible before him, his bare backside resting on the smoothest brick floor he had seen outside of a public swimming pool. Liam clutched his good knee to his chest. The other one was having none of it. Every time he attempted to move, a searing pain would engulf his every sense.

Shite!

Out of the corner of his eye, he noticed a steel cabinet, stationed beside him. Liam reached out and wrapped his hand around a bandage and slide-rule which lay fortuitously atop. He braced his knee with the slide-rule and used the bandage to bind, in the vane hope that he might be able to put a little weight on his burning limb.

His teeth chattered as he tried to think. Glancing down, Liam observed two lines of channel gratings, still wet from a recent cleaning. His eyes then panned left and right as he took in his current environment. One whole wall was lined with steel drawers. They stood three high and seven wide. He estimated that each box was approximately two feet square.

Liam was beginning to come round a little more when his gaze was drawn to the metal table, resting at the heart of the room. Iron bolts pinned it to the floor and atop of it was something that looked very much like a body bag.

A memory jarred his brain, then another and another, until his whole mind flooded with incoherent snapshots of prior events. He could not understand anything he saw and found himself powerless to stop it. His mind took in more and more memories, until he felt he could no longer weather the intense confusion. With his hands pressed tightly to his ears, he sought to prevent the inescapable eruption. At this point, his mind did not so much explode as *implode*. All the new information that his brain had taken in was now shot at great speed into the relevant slots of his temporal lobe.

As swiftly as it had begun, it ceased.

The gears in his head started to slow down; his muscles began to relax; his breathing slowed as he took in long, slow, deep breaths. As his eyes came gently back into focus, he carefully removed his hands from his ears.

Raising his head, he stared again, directly at what was most definitely a body bag; *his* body bag. All his memories were back where they should be and he could remember the whole sordid story. A light had come on in the upstairs regions of his brain and he now recalled why he was there.

His eyes were then drawn down to his frosty feet. One big toe was black, through lack of blood. The numbness was sore but once he left that cold place and the feeling started to return to him, he was going to be in a great deal more pain than he had ever experienced before.

Pulling himself carefully to his good foot and bracing himself against the steel cabinet, he scanned the rest of the room. When he found what he was looking for, he hobbled inexpertly towards the far wall, grasping onto anything stable enough to sustain his strained body. There was one moment where he had shifted his weight onto a trolly, only for it to roll away from him, causing his meagre nine stone body to crumple onto the wet floor. Liam screamed again in foul-mouthed protestation as he came into sharp contact with the brutal floor.

Glancing upwards, he saw a desk with the clear plastic drawers that had attracted his attention. He reached out and wrapped his numbing fingers around one leg of the desk and pulled himself towards it, cringing as he did. Propping himself up against the desk, he breathed heavily and hauled out each drawer in turn, the contents being strewn about the floor, until Liam found what he was searching for.

Wrapping a rubber bind around his upper arm and tying it off, his thumb pressed down on the syringe as the unplumbed dose of morphine was driven into his swollen vein. He closed his eyes and his breathing slowed to what might be passed for relative normalcy. In a few minutes, he would feel like himself again.

A short '*bzzz*' came from outside the room. A door had just been opened. Liam jumped instantly into the crouch position, the influence of his own adrenaline distracting him from his bitter pain, if not actually relieving it any. Whatever was about to occur, he knew he would regret it the next day.

When the trainee doctor stepped into the room, his eyes were immediately drawn to the empty body bag. The next thing that grabbed his attention was the young, naked boy, crouching under the desk whom the novice was quite certain had been dead only ten minutes before.

Liam rushed at the newcomer like a scrawny Quasimodo and pinned him against the wall. Gripping the unsuspecting student by the throat, Liam eyed him up and down. A manic grin crossing his face, Liam whispered into the young man's trembling ear, 'I need you to do me a wee favour.'

*

When he limped out of the hospital on his stolen crutches, Liam was dressed up in the novice's blue scrubs, worn under a long black coat. Tipping the also newly acquired charcoal-grey flat-cap over his face, he breathed in the fresh air and made his way back into the world.

The Likely Lads and Ladette

Six Months earlier...

The engine screamed in torment as the stolen Mercedes Benz A-Class sped down the old single-track road, east of Kilmarnock, at hitherto unheard-of speed for that particular byway. Most of the edifices that whirred past were either farmhouses, storehouses, greenhouses or henhouses; excepting one ancient ramshackle outhouse. That did not mean, however, that there would be no people about.

William Fionnlagh[1] Macrae, Liam to his mates, stared with intense concentration in his furrowed brow, through the rain-sodden windscreen. He was sixteen years young

---

[1] Pron.: f-yorn-uch

with short brown hair and had just bitten off a little more than he could chew. His knuckles burned as his hands clenched around the steering wheel, the rhythmic vibrations pulsing through his body. Unsure of foot, he pressed down on the accelerator only as much as he dared.

There was limited entertainment made available for post-millennials in this small town. Therefore, not half an hour earlier, Liam had found himself unable to resist lifting the dramatic dusky-grey Mercedes from a badly lit alley. The unfortunate and oblivious owner had abandoned their pride and joy with the keys still resting in the slot, as they briefly stepped into a local chip shop to retrieve their dinner. It was not something that Liam made a habit of but, he had to admit, it was something he had started doing more and more, these days.

He let his eyes rise from the road for the briefest of seconds. He caught a glimpse of a One Series BMW keeping speed, not half a car length behind him, and an Alfa Romeo Giulietta behind that. Liam allowed his foot to press down a little more than he honestly felt comfortable with and accelerated steadily away.

The cars twisted and turned with the slim tarmac road as the three adolescent motorists held on for dear life; Liam scanning the road in desperation, as he searched for anything coming towards them.

A drone flew high above, rising and descending as the camera shot required, the person on the other end intent on capturing the three cars as they played the country backroads.

Liam retrieved his phone from out of his pocket, pressed his thumb against the secure lock and threw it onto the dashboard. Shouting above the noise of the engine, Liam yelled, 'Hey Google, call Sparks.' As the phone started to dial, Liam quickly pressed the loudspeaker icon and waited for a response.

The phone was answered by a girl of the same age as Liam. "Sup?' Sparks asked, distractedly.

'Hey honey,' Liam answered, 'do you think you've got enough footage for the film, yet. I don't think we can keep this up for much longer; someone's bound to be walking their dog or something. I'm not up for a manslaughter charge on top of theft and reckless driving.'

'Almost there,' Sparks replied. 'Another few minutes and we should be sorted.'

'Not sure we have that amount of time,' Liam sighed as he was distracted by some blue and white flashing lights coming up quickly behind them. He looked ahead again, to see more alarming lights on the horizon. 'Let's just say we have some company.'

'Dammit,' Sparks expleted down the phone, 'right. I'll lock all this down on my end. You just make sure all three of you get out of this in one piece.'

'Right you are,' Liam replied as Sparks hung up the phone. He grabbed it from the dashboard where it had been sliding back and forth and slipped it into his pocket, once again as he pulled the zip tight.

With the dexterity of a kite in search of prey, the drone banked southwards and absconded, bearing towards the nine-street village of Crookedholm; so named because the *crooked* river Irvine has, over the years, formed a smooth *holm* land.

Where the drone hastened, Liam tapered off, the other two drivers following suit.

Liam's eyes searched the surrounding area, his mind set on one thing and one thing only; any means of escape. Ahead of him and to his left, an open gate came into view. Signalling to the other two in their pre-agreed way, by tapering along the right bank of the road and tapping the brake as lightly as if a feather had landed on it.

With everyone aware of what was about to transpire, the open gate arrived on their left and Liam swung through it with as much force as he could muster, while still ensuring all four wheels remained steadfast and shot into the hayfield, beyond.

He had barely travelled twenty meters before Liam felt the car blaspheme as one of his springs snapped, causing the front driver's wheel to sink and get wedged in the drowning muck. Liam was left hanging, the car's back passenger wheel spinning in midair as the right-hand one spat out mud and crop seedlings, behind him.

When Liam squinted in his rear-view mirror, he saw that Shug, who had been driving the stolen BMW, was in the same sorry state that Liam was, having had to slam on his breaks before he ploughed into the backside of the marooned Merc. The stout ginger-haired boy was giving one of the wheels a good hard kick.

The third of the young drivers, Angus, who had initially been enjoying the Alfa Romeo, had tried to take the turn at too great a speed and had ended his failed manoeuvre turning the car over onto its roof.

A twang of guilt and fear flashed through Liam's mind before he allowed a sigh of relief escape his lips, as he caught sight of his careless friend scrambling out from the upturned vehicle and departing the scene like he was otherwise destined for the electric chair. His shoulder-length brown hair flew up behind him as *he* flew away.

Liam thought this was a good decision on Angus' part and made to do the same. Unclasping his seatbelt and kicking open the door, Liam swung his legs out onto the muddy farm ground that had brought an end to their playtime. He looked again at Shug who had come to the same decision and together they made a consensual ruling to run for it, south-west.

The persistent scolding of the displeased officers echoed as they tried to foil the boy's escape but the two uneducated delinquents made no attempt to follow the officers' wishes.

Both, the police and the three boys held opposing beliefs as to how this night was supposed to end. The boys felt that the night would be a good one if they could leave these unfit policemen behind them and press on through the newly planted fields to a place of safety and afterwards, home. The police thought that the only way *their* night was going to work out was if they managed to grab the three young scallywags and drag them down to the station for questioning.

What it would eventually come down to was force of will and waist size. Liam had more self-will than most of the people he knew and believed with unequivocal sincerity that he was quicker than any patrolman. He was certainly satisfied that his waistline was a good deal less than those particular officers of the law, mild, if not exactly hot at his heel. Strong will and physical fitness, that was what was going to get the boys out of the mess they were in.

Just ahead of Liam and Shug, a fence appeared through the darkness. They headed straight for it, having no idea as to where Angus had raced off to.

Liam hurdled the fence in one go. Shug was not so lucky. He did not so much jump over the fence as crash straight into it. What made matters worse was that it not only had a thin curl of barbed wire hemmed along the top but the wire it was wrapped around was also electrified. Every time Shug attempted to unhook his jumper from the barbed wire, one hundred and twenty milliamps earthed through him. By the time he managed to free himself and clamber over the fence without too many unpleasant jolts through the tips of his fingers (or his unmentionables, as he swung one leg over and then the other), the police were almost on top of them.

'Come on,' Liam shouted at the justly upset Shug who had an unnatural tingling in the sensitive areas of his boxershorts. He would never try to climb over an electric fence again, so long as he lived.

'I'm coming, alright!' Shug yelled back. 'Just you get going. There's no need for them to catch the both of us.'

'I don't want them to catch either of us,' Liam protested. 'Will you just get a move on. I think we can get through those trees at the other end of the field and then onto the bypass. Once we're across that, we're home and dry. Plenty of places to hide out.'

'Let's hope you're right,' Shug prayed, 'otherwise we're done for.'

The two boys ran through the second field as fast as their legs would carry them. Each of them felt independently like their hearts were going to explode. Still, the thumpity-thump pulsing through their bodies caused an adrenaline spike which kept them moving on, even as their breathing quickened.

Liam remembered as he ran that he had left his bottle of juice in the car. *Shite*, Liam thought. That was not good. Chances were that their fingerprints and DNA could both be divulged from that. *The same could be said for the sweaty grip on the steering wheel*, Liam thought to himself as the F-word repeated itself numerous times in his head.

There was no time to worry about that now. First, they had to make their escape. Then and only then would they have the time to figure out what to do next.

As they reached the end of the second field, Liam spotted a wooden style and directed Shug towards it. They made short work of the steps and were over and at the edge of the dual carriageway in a matter of seconds. Stopping just short of being on the road itself, the boys held their gazes right as they looked for an opening. The shouts and whistles of the police as they arrived at the edge of the adjacent field were getting worryingly clear.

Before too long, Liam saw an opening in the traffic and took off. Shug followed in hot pursuit and they both arrived at the central barrier at the same time, just as an eighteen-wheeler came hurtling past them at fifty miles an hour.

'That was a bit of a close one,' Shug remarked.

Liam scowled at his friend. 'I hope Angus is having an easier time than us, that's all I can say.'

'He went off like he had a rocket up his arse,' cried Shug, 'without so much as a by your leave. He'll be fine, don't you worry. He's got a lucky streak, that one.'

'He'd better have,' Liam sighed. 'Now, let's get across the other side before those fine officers find a way through, themselves.'

'Lead the way, captain,' Shug saluted.

'None of that,' Liam scolded. 'Let's just go.'

Again, the two boys stared down the traffic as it hurried past them, this time looking down to the left. Again, an opening was found and again, they ran. They kept on running until they could go no further.

The boys ended up in a dark alley, leading through to the cemetery. They were only a short walk through the Kay Park to get to their respective homes; Liam one way and Shug, the other. They rested against an oversized gravestone as they regained some of their breath and allowed their hearts to stop pounding.

'I think we lost them,' Shug gasped.

'Oh, nice one,' Liam proclaimed, 'now you've said that, they'll saunter round that corner any second.'

'Didn't know you were the superstitious type,' Shug inquired, wheezing as he searched around his pockets for his blue inhaler.

'I'm not,' Liam confirmed, 'but what I do believe in is Murphy's Law, so don't go around tempting fate by letting phrases like that out of your mouth.'

'Please yourself,' sighed Shug. 'I'm away to get myself a wash and some shut-eye. I'll see you the morrow.'

'Fair enough,' sighed Liam. 'Mind and keep an eye out over the next wee while. I don't know how long it takes for fingerprints or DNA results to come through but when they do, we want to be ready for whatever happens.'

'Right you are, bud. Catch you on the flip side.'

With that, Shug made his way home, towards his bed.

Liam looked right, towards where his own bed lay, and sighed, again. Lazily putting one foot in front of the other, he plodded off in the direction of home.

On arrival, Liam made his way up the graffiti-tagged concrete stairs that smelled, stiffly of other people's urine. At the top, he turned right and entered the second flat on his left which was adorned with a cardboard square where a small, frosted window used to be.

He locked the door behind him and went straight up the stairs of his mother's two up, one down flat. After briefly popping his head around her bedroom door to make sure she was no worse than usual, he fell straight into his own bed and drifted off, into the land of nod.

He dreamed of many things that night, none of which made any sense to him. There was an old railway line, a masquerade mask and a hell of a lot of blood.

Some Mothers do Have Them

Liam's body thrashed around as the intangible dreams became more and more vivid. When he awoke, he was dripping in his own sweat, so much so that his wafer-thin duvet was soaked through. He could not remember much of the unpleasant nocturnal images, yet he was bequeathed an unwanted sensation of anguish that still lingered. Even if he could recall, he would have been hard pressed to find any manner of significance in his visions. Liam was not one to believe in the veracity of dreams, which countless others were all too quick to put meaning to, but the uncomfortable night terrors brought with them an all too real feeling of foreboding.

As he showered, Liam thought back on the previous night's mischief and, given all the facts, he did not think he had any hope of reprieve whatsoever. He would surely go down for his recklessness. He was already on two strikes and if they managed to pin Liam to this latest mess then he would surely be destined for HMYOI[2] Polmont, the local detention centre. Not just for a weekend visit to scare him straight but the real deal. Eighteen to twenty-four months of hell; his solicitor and social worker had both been quite clear about that. Apparently, the judge had been severe and colloquially verbal on the matter.

This was not a happy state of affairs. The last thing Liam wanted was to get banged up in one of those places. They were filled to the brim with a strong cocktail of thieves, scammers and predators. Someone like Liam, young, naïve and naught but skin and bone, would have a hard time on the inside.

---

[2] He Majesty's Young Offenders Institution

If it came down to it then he would rather run away and hide out somewhere for the foreseeable future; maybe work his way up to the isle of Lewis where his aunt Mhari lived.

This would be difficult, he had to admit. Liam had no real money to speak of and the declining state of his mother's health was a constant concern. The doctors were trying everything they could but her condition kept declining. Matters had gotten to the point where she was now completely bedbound and could barely get any word out but for a strained asthmatic whisper.

Liam's father, on the other hand, had left when Liam was seven. Liam could not remember much about what had transpired for his old man to just up and leave yet that was exactly what he had done. The only memory that Liam still had of that day was his father kneeling down and placing a kind hand on Liam's shoulder, before saying, 'Look after your mother, son. Sorry I can't stay.' Then he stood up, collected his one suitcase from the side of the road and walked smartly away into ever fading memory.

Liam's mother had cried, although, looking back on it now, she had seemed more resolute than sad. Maybe she had chosen to bear the weight of their loss so as not to scare the younger Liam; perhaps. It certainly did not take her long to revert back to using her maiden name, obliging Liam do the same.

Liam could not remember his mother ever working. She had always claimed to be on benefits but being so ill she had not been out the house long enough to sign on and Liam had not been able to find any sign of a docket or even a letter in regard to what specific benefit she was getting or how much it was. He had made enquiries at the dole office but the lady behind the desk had been unwilling to pass out any information on anyone unless she had a power of attorney sitting in front of her.

It was all very strange but the payments kept coming, every week without fail. He had tried to track the routing number but the bank had been unable to determine the name on the outgoing account. That's what they had said that to Liam, at any rate. Whether or not it was true was another matter. Liam had decided that it did not make a difference where her payments were coming from, just so long as they continued.

None of this, however, would solve Liam's current dilemma. With no money for himself, he was not likely to get very far. If he were to simply steal whatever he needed along the way, he would surely start to get noticed and anyone who might be looking for him would eventually track his movements. He was in a sticky bind and no mistake.

This was something he would have to think on a bit more.

As all this was running through his mind, he dried himself, dressed and made his way downstairs, popping his head in to check his mother was alright. Liam then went through to the kitchen, popped the kettle on the gas ring and pulled a half-washed mug from the draining board.

Listening to the low hum of the water starting to boil, still pondering what he might do about his grim predicament, Liam became aware of a ringing sound. It was the front door. Liam left the kettle to do its job and walked through the hallway to the front door of the flat and peered through the eyehole. Outside, there stood a sizeable gentleman with a shaved head and a prominent, mountain man beard.

'Shite,' Liam cursed aloud and opened the door. 'What is it *you* want?' he growled at the man who stood before him.

'You know what I want,' the man replied. 'Listen, I only want to see her. I'm concerned, that's all.'

'It wouldn't matter if you were the Pope, himself, you're not going up and she can't come down; so, you're buggered.'

'Look son...' the man started.

'Don't call me son,' Liam growled again. 'You lost the right to fatherhood nine years ago when you walked out on us. You can't just keep turning up here, month after month and expect anything to have changed from the last time I slammed the door in your face.' Liam tried to close said door but a wide boot was shoved securely in the way.

'You don't know the full story, son. Just let me explain.'

Liam fumed. 'I told you not to call me that,' he yelled as he kicked his father in the shin and drove the door home, slipping the chain into its slot and turning the mortice for good measure.

Thirty seconds past before the shadow of the unwelcome patriarch passed over the one unbroken frosted glass window, head bowed in shame; or maybe desperation. Either way, he was gone. He would be back again in a few weeks, of course, although Liam could not figure out why. *Why, if he wanted to spend so much time there, did he ever leave in the first place?* But that was a mystery he did not care about solving. His father had left them and that was that. He had made it quite clear, back then, that he had no interest in Liam or his mother and that was the way things were. *Sod him.*

Liam made his way back through to the kitchen just as the kettle was starting to squeal. He made himself a strong cup of tea and a couple of slices of toast and sat himself down in the small sittingroom. As he pressed the red button on the remote control, the television flickered into life and the Reporting Scotland newsroom came into view. Liam did not watch the news all too often but today he was interested to see if there was anything on there about last night's events.

There was. Item six, of the seven that made it to air, was all about the chase. A Police Inspector was interviewed as well as a couple of others who had seen the boys jacking the cars in the first place. Rough sketches of the three boys were postered and a request for any information regarding the three juvenile delinquents was sent out around the country. Things were moving oddly fast.

Liam had to admit that it was uncharacteristic for the police to be that much on the ball. Something was not right but Liam could not put his finger on what that could be. It normally took a few days for this kind of press release to come out and they rarely had witnesses or photofits by that point. That sort of thing usually came later, along with the DNA results and the fingerprinting.

Liam had the distinct feeling that the whole world was about to come crashing down around him. It was then that he remembered Angus and how he and Shug had not heard so much as a peep from their friend since he had fled, leaving them alone and twiddling their thumbs. Liam pulled his phone out from his pocket and brought up the home screen. 'Hey Google, call Angus,'

41

he called out, remembering that he would have to give Sparks a call back, too.

The phone started ringing. But, after three unanswered attempts, he was distracted by another ring from the door.

'What does he want this time?' Liam sighed, more than a little irritated, as he walked, leisurely towards the front door to the flat.

Are You Being Served a Warrant

Liam opened the front door to the flat and stared, in disbelief at the two large gentlemen who darkened his doorway. Each of them was almost properly shaven and a good three feet taller than Liam was. You might say that they were built like the proverbial brick outhouse. The hulks wore suits that were nicer than any which Liam would be able to afford but not as nice as if they had been made specially. Under their suit jackets, they both wore crisp white shirts but had chosen, for some reason to forget about putting on a tie. They had gone for the open top button look. It said, to Liam at least, that these men were professional but not to the detriment of being comfortable.

'Can I help you?' Liam asked after a few seconds of uncomfortable silence.

The bulkier and more serious looking of the two, a good ten years older than the other, looked Liam gruffly up and down. His nose was turned up like someone had just let one go. 'William Macrae?' he asked.

'Yes,' Liam confirmed, his melancholy rising as he witnessed the two giants at his door.

The man smiled. 'Mr Ferguson would like a wee word wi ye,' he continued. It was not a request and Liam got the distinct impression that declining the invitation would not be the best idea if he wished to stay healthy.

'Of course,' Liam replied. 'Just tell me where and when and I'll make sure to be there.'

The smaller of the two large men gave a short, uncomical smile. 'Here,' he said, 'and now.'

With that, the two men stepped aside and a clean-shaven older gentleman of around sixty years in age, moved into view. His hair was expertly combed and he wore a suit which was far superior to the ones his emissaries wore. This suit was not any Marks and Sparks bulk job; this was a Slater's, hand crafted, made-to-measure, work of art in fabric form. Over the suit, the older gentleman wore a camel coloured, woollen overcoat. Liam suspected, by the look of the man, that it may well have been made from an actual camel.

'Good morning,' Ferguson addressed Liam, pausing as he awaited a response from the boy. Liam was still in shock. When it became apparent the expected response was never going to arrive, the man continued, 'Well,' he said, 'are you not going to invite us in? Ron, here, has a spot of lumbago and the cold air does nothing to improve his mood.'

Liam cast his gaze back to the larger of the two men and gulped. 'Certainly,' he stuttered, 'come on in.'

Mr Ferguson smiled, showing some internal amusement across his rough and battle-scarred face which held more marks and potholes than the A8, near to Paisley. Followed by Ron and the other large gentleman, whom Liam would later discover was called Charlie, Ferguson walked through to the sittingroom. He looked around the room, taking in the nineteen-seventies architecture, embroidered with nineteen-eighties décor. The carpet was the newest thing in the room, having been fitted in the spring of ninety-one. Ferguson nodded to himself and sat down in the single armchair that sat beside the three-bar electric fire.

Liam was more than uncomfortable. The name Willie Ferguson, often referred to as *'The Big Yin'*, was a concern to many people. Those whom it did not concern, either did not know who he was or managed to keep well enough out of his watchful eye for it not to be an issue. Liam had most definitely heard the name and would have been shaking in his boots if he had been wearing any. If he had been wearing wellingtons then he would have had warm, wet feet.

Eventually, Liam managed to get his voice to work and asked the all-important question. 'How do you take your tea?'

Ferguson, who had been admiring Liam's mother's old needlework which hung on the wall, above the fake fire's mantle, said that he would have milk and one sugar.

'Just milk in mine,' added Charlie in a rough, raspy voice from just behind Liam's left ear, 'I'm sweet enough.'

'And I'll huv a coo and two,' finished Ron.

Liam paused. 'You're not from around here, are you?'

'Ron, here, grew up in a small fishing town called Buckie,' Ferguson answered, 'just East of Elgin.'

'That's no' gang tae be a problem, is it?' Ron inquired, spitting pure Doric.

'Certainly not,' Liam responded, swiftly. 'Spent some lovely holidays up that way when I was a kid.'

'When was that,' Charlie grinned, 'last week?'

'Aye, yer still no' lang aff the line, noo, are ye?'

'Sorry?' Liam asked, getting worried.

'He said,' Charlie assisted, 'that you're *still* a kid, so don't *kid* yourself into thinking otherwise.'

'Look, I didn't mean anything by it,' Liam pleaded, a tear forming in his eye.

'Come on now, lads. Leave the boy alone,' Ferguson interjected, coming to Liam's rescue. 'He's going to go into the kitchen now and make us all a nice cuppa to warm us up. Maybe a couple of biscuits, if he has any.'

'If he has any sense,' Charlie added, chuckling, with menace.

Liam took this as his chance for a breather and quickly darted through the open, beaded door that led to the kitchen. By the time he got there, he could not remember for love or money what Ron and Charlie had asked for in their tea. In the end, he made Ferguson's the way he wanted and brought the other two mugs out and simply laid them out on the coffee table with a bowl of sugar and a bottle of milk, unopened.

'The cream topper's mine,' stated Ron, who managed to grab the milk bottle first.

He cracked the gold foil lid with his thumb and poured a healthy amount into his mug.

After the tea ceremony had been completed, Liam stood with his hands clasped in front of him as he waited for Ferguson to explain why he had decided to pay him a visit.

When Ferguson had finished his warm beverage, he rested the cup and saucer, which Liam was at least smart enough to dig out of the cupboard for the man, onto his knee and held it there with fore and thumb.

'Now, Mr Macrae,' Ferguson began, 'I understand that you were in possession of a vehicle, last night, which did not belong to you.'

Liam did not know what to say to this, so he said nothing.

'I'll take your lack of defence as a confession,' Ferguson continued, 'coupled with the fact that it was my Mercedes you borrowed for your fun time. I am a very diligent man, Mr Macrae and had the good fortitude to have a couple of cameras installed for insurance purposes. I guess we're seeing the fruit of that action, right now.'

Liam gulped for the second time and tried to grovel his way out of the truly dire situation in which he found himself. He said he was sorry; promised that he had not known who the car had belonged to; begged for forgiveness; and offered to find a way to pay off the damage.

'I do not want your money, Mr Macrae,' Ferguson replied. 'I can well afford to pay for the minimal damage that you miraculously inflicted on it.'

Liam breathed a sigh of relief.

Ferguson continued. 'I have also informed the police that *we* will not be pressing charges.' He looked at Ron and Charlie.

'We?' Liam sighed. 'Let me guess, the BMW and the Alpha were yours?'

'Aye, they were that,' answered Ron. Charlie merely growled.

'I'm really sorry,' was all that Liam could muster.

'There's no need to be sorry,' Ferguson went on, 'because you're going to make it up to us, aren't you?'

Liam felt his stomach drop and his heart stop for the briefest of seconds which felt like a lifetime. He gulped for the third time and certainly not the last. 'Of course, Mr Ferguson, sir,' Liam replied, understanding all too well that his life had just taken a severe downward spiral.

Early Doors

Liam walked down the street, hands thrust in his pockets, his hood up over his head and pulled down to the level of his eyebrows. As his teeth chattered, Liam marched on toward a place where he knew that nobody would come looking for him.

The day had not gone as planned. Ups and downs, certainly. It had been a relief that the police were not going to be involved in the previous night's joyride but that moment of reprieve had been short lived. He was now in the pocket of Willie Ferguson, one of the hardest and certainly most ruthless men in the area. The rumour was that he had been involved in racketeering, extortion, and the dealing of drugs since before he turned eighteen. Ferguson had been one to watch, even then. Now, he was one to watch out for, so that you could be sure to run away in the opposite direction.

Liam had not been given the option to run. He had planned to have himself a fun night and had ended up making a serious mistake. If he had taken any other of the forty cars that were parked on that street, instead of the fancy Mercedes then, yes, he would have been in trouble but that would have been with the police. He would have been charged, he would have pled guilty and he would have done his time in the detention centre. A year to eighteen months later, he would have been out, free and clear. That is not to say that he would not have hated every second of being confined there but at least he would not have been in debt to Ferguson.

This was his worst nightmare. When someone like Ferguson gets you then it's incredibly difficult to find a way out again.

That evening of reckless amusement may just have changed the whole course of his life and not for the better. Things were bad and Liam could not see any way out of it. He would have to have a good hard think about matters and see if he could figure out a way to break free from Ferguson's grasp.

Which was why he was marching down the road, hood up and head down. He knew the perfect place to hide away for a few hours and it was undeniably a place where nobody, not even those who truly knew him (*especially those who knew him*) would ever believe he was holding up. He did not particularly wish to go there but needs must as the devil drives; and the devil was surely driving him demented today. This was the worst situation Liam had ever been in and he had to find a way out of it before things went too far. When you got someone like Ferguson involved in anything then it was a sure sign that something would eventually fall hard on your head. Ferguson would be fine and dandy, of course, but the plebs like Liam would always be the ones to come up on charges or, even worse, go down in the dirt; a whole six feet down. That, of course, was if they ever found your body.

Liam could not imagine anyone choosing to get into this life but there were many who had done just that. People would see the more successful of the gangsters in their fancy cars, wearing their luxurious watches and their incredibly expensive suits, and think to themselves, *that is what I want in life*. And some had managed it. Most had not. A lot of kids who joined up, as it were, thought that selling drugs to their friends would eventually bring a step up to other, more profitable areas. They were taken in by the supposed glamorous lifestyle and were hooked. That is to say that they would, if moderately successful at profiteering off their mates and always took their cash on delivery, be allowed a small amount of what was known as 'tick'. This meant that their supervisor, usually termed as 'dealer' would give the boy or girl a certain amount of product with the expectation that when they had sold it, they would then bring their dealer's share to him (or her). If this did not run smoothly then the profits would be extracted in other ways and nobody wanted to go down that road.

That was basically where Liam was at that moment. He had made his mistake and was now to pay for it in some way or another. Ferguson had not explained what Liam would be expected to do, only that he was to jump when told or he would be in the dirt with no say in the matter.

Liam did not like the sound of that. He had his suspicions, of course, about what he may be asked to do. He would either be made to become a full-time thief or be forced to sell drugs. Neither of these options had any appeal for him but if he had the choice then he would surely want to keep as far away from the drug scene as he possibly could.

Liam was a good thief, he knew that, but he had, up till that point, only participated in such a way that was fun for him. He did it for amusement. Liam would steal a car to have the thrill of racing it up and down the backstreets; he would pickpocket a wallet or purse so that he could pay for concert tickets or a night down the pub; or he would pinch tobacco from the shops because he wanted to partake in that common pastime of getting high.

This was a bit of a misnomer, if truth be told. When smoking cannabis, the last place it got you was high. Alcohol is an upper; cocaine is an upper; ecstasy is an upper; but cannabis is a downer. You simply get very mellow. All your muscles relax and you drift away as like sleep. It was well known to be a relaxant but it also helped with pain and was a natural anti-inflammatory. It had even been shown to have its uses in the care of people with parkinson's or glaucoma. Why it was still illegal was a mystery to Liam, especially if there had been no recorded deaths because of its use, unless you count one of Willie Nelson's friends being crushed by a runaway bale.

Basically, Liam had got himself into quite a bit of a bind and if Ferguson had managed to find his way to Liam's mother's flat so quickly after the event then Shug and Angus would certainly be next. Whether they would be visited, in the same manner as Liam had been or if some other fate was in store for them, Liam did not know but either way, this was not a good time to have been involved in that particular car chase. Sparks might be alright, not having been there in person, but maybe, if someone knew that she hung out with the boys on a regular basis, they might deduce that she was probably involved. If someone spotted the drone then her name would most assuredly pop up at some point.

Sparks, who wore her long black hair in dreadlocks, was one of the brightest in the school and had the grades to go on to any elite university of her choosing but education came all too easily for her. When she was told something, she remembered it; when she read something, the image of the page would be burned into her brain forever; and anything that she heard, she could listen back to as if it were a recording. Liam and the others always used to give her a ribbing, saying that she must have been some kind of governmental experiment. Sparks did not take too kindly to this but never got angry. 'Who knows,' she would say, starting at almost a whisper and gaining edge until she was halfway to shouting, 'maybe I am. Maybe I am a robot in disguise and I've been sent here to spy on you three lazy gobshites.'

This would make them all laugh and smile. Sparks had been one of the gang ever since they were but six years old. Friends for life, the lot of them. Anything one did, they all did. There was nothing that had even come close to changing that or even challenging it. They were all the very best of pals and any ribbing was meant and taken for what it was; a lively unharmful joke between friends.

The last thing that Liam wanted was for the previous night's escapades to corrupt their friendships or put any of them into danger. Liam had known all of them for all of his recollected life and they were the closest thing he had to siblings. He would do anything for them but currently they all seemed to be in a pile of trouble that they might not be able to escape.

This was all very troubling so, when he reached the front door of the Ginger Nightcap, the place he did not want to be and where nobody would look to find him, he stepped over the threshold without any qualms.

On the other side of the door was an old-time pub; what people usually refer to as an 'old man pub'. It was of simple design. There was a bar along the right-hand wall which held many bottles of spirits, seated on the shelves behind the barman who, keeping with tradition, was polishing a whisky glass with a bar towel. The barman, Tommy 'One

Thumb' MacInnes, was in his seventies; Liam did not know how old exactly but he was certainly a mighty resilient septuagenarian.

The Ginger Nightcap was a simple place where people went to drink a quiet nip, each for their own personal reasons. It was also a *hard* pub. The men who frequented this place of refuge were no soft breed. Each and every one of them had a reputation and were respected for it inside and outside of the convivial sanctuary. The owner had made it his business to ensure that everyone who entered would, if they obeyed the few simple rules, be treated with respect and even kindness. *This is the purpose of a public house*; the owner had said. He had said it each and every day to Liam for the first seven years of his life. This is because, the owner of the Ginger Nightcap was, in point of fact, Liam's own father, Cameron William

Buchanan. It has already been said that Liam's mother, on splitting from her husband of ten years, decided not to keep using her married name but instead reverted to her father's surname of Macrae. This was not done officially and so, legally Liam was a Buchanan, too.

At the end of the bar, fastened to the wall, was an open cupboard which held a dart board. All the darts were kept behind the bar, however, until requested for a match, just on the off chance that there would come a disagreement and someone would find one protruding from their eye. It had unfortunately happened in the past and Liam's father had no wish for anything like that to occur again. When Mr Buchanan made a decision, it was followed and there was no soul disrespectful enough to disagree with him on any subject. Nobody except Tommy One Thumb. They had been best of friends for years and there was nobody whom Liam's father trusted more in this world. Each of the two men knew each other's minds in their entirety and no secret was ever kept between the pair. Tommy had been like an uncle to Liam, once, but that was some time ago.

Lining the left-hand wall, were some booths where people could sit and talk or eat or do whatever business it was that they needed to do. The booths even had curtains that could be pulled across to give the occupants some privacy, if required. In the centre of the room, there sat a few small tables where three or four people could sit around, comfortably.

Beyond the bar, in a smaller room, there was a top-of-the-line pool table which was a popular place for the locals to meet. All-in-all, the Ginger Nightcap was a pleasant place to have a cheeky glass or two of an evening. Little trouble was ever started within those walls and such trouble that did occur was dealt with quickly and effectively.

At that moment in time, however, the bar was empty but for Tommy the barman. Liam ignored everything in the room except the empty bar stool closest to the window and perched himself on it. He grabbed Tommy's attention and the aging but not incapable barman wandered over in his direction. A large smile appeared on his face when he realised who had just graced the threshold with his appearance.

'Liam,' he said, jovially, 'is that yourself?'

'Aye, Tommy. It is indeed.' Liam returned a smile. He had always liked Tommy and saw no point in dealing out scorn on him. It was Liam's father who had left and that was no fault of Tommy's. He hadn't even been around at the time.

'Well, hang my nuts with a rusty hook,' Tommy continued, uncouthly. 'As I live and breathe, it's good to see your face again.'

'It's certainly been a while,' agreed Liam. 'I don't think I've been in here since I was seven.'

'Not quite,' Tommy corrected. 'You came in here once on your thirteenth, I think it was. Stayed for an hour, had a fight with your old man about something or other and went off home to your mothers. Never saw you again, after that.'

'Ah, yes. I remember,' Liam recalled.

'Well, it's all in the past,' Tommy soothed. 'A surprise to see you now, though. I'm afraid, however, that you're father's not here, this afternoon. So, that'll be a wasted trip for you.'

'I thought he wouldn't be,' Liam replied. 'He's usually off visiting Aunt Mhari, in Shawbost at the weekends. I saw him before he left, anyway. I only came here today to get away from others.'

'Really,' inquired Tommy, 'and who might this be?'

'Nothing for you to worry yourself about,' Liam answered as he browsed the fifty shades of the Ginger Nightcap's amber nectar which graced the back of the bar. 'Pour us both a double of yon Auchentoshan forty-two, will you. And put in on my father's tab. I feel a well-earned nip is in order.' Liam stepped to the door and turned the lock, pulling down the blinds of the currently empty bar to stop anyone outside from looking in.

'The nineteen sixty-five bottle?' Tommy grinned, 'at two hundred and forty-three pounds a nip? You can tell him yourself,' he added as he cracked open the unsoiled bottle and poured two glasses of the expensively delicate whisky. He passed one over to Liam, raised his own in the air and paid their grace. 'Slàinte mhath[3],' he announced as Liam raised his own in respect, nodding in reverential[4] agreement.

Although Liam himself had been born and raised just south of the central belt, his father's family had come from the islands off the west coast. This is why he had a Gaelic middle name which translated into Findley and why, when toasting good health, his family and dearest friends would always use the Gaelic. No other use of the language was known to Liam. He was sure that his father had the Gaelic and that he had probably taught it to Tommy at some point over the years but Liam had never seen the need for it. His father had told him once that it was more important that Liam was able to speak

---

[3] Pron.: slan-jé-vah
[4] The enjoyment of good whisky is considered a pious experience in Scotland.

a language that others could not; the police for example, or the English.

Boy and man chatted convivially for a time as they enjoyed their once-in-a-lifetime sup of the special uisge na beatha[5], which meant 'water of life'.

*

Tommy had tried again to discover what was troubling Liam, during their time together, but the boy was in no mood to reveal any details. Liam simply said that he had found himself in a slight bind but that he would figure a way out of it, not to worry. This did nothing to reassure the old barman who had seen many people coming in and out of the Ginger Nightcap, over the years, who had worn the same look as Liam had

---

[5] Often shortened to *uisge beatha*

on his face when he had first walked into the pub. The look told Tommy that something bad had happened but if he could not get any details out of the boy then there was little that he could do about it. He would, of course, let Mr Buchanan know that his son had been in and that he, Tommy, was a bit concerned for the boy but, beyond that, there was nothing much he could do to help Liam. He really wished that the boy trusted him enough to at least share his grievance even if he did not wish any assistance with the matter. He would just have to do his best to keep a look out for the boy and a few questions, here and there, was not out of the question. He would not press Liam into saying more but Tommy decided that he would look about and see what he could learn. He had a lot of ears in that town.

*

When Liam had finished his drink, he thanked Tommy for his time and walked out of the Ginger Nightcap, happier but no more sure about what he was going to do about his perilous situation. He supposed that he would have to simply wait and see what it was that Ferguson wanted him to do. Liam was sure that he would not personally see Ferguson again, certainly not for a good long while. This was a blessing, Liam thought but when he realised that he would probably have to deal with Ron and Charlie instead, he felt quite sick. They would not be easy to work with and would likely snap Liam like a twig if anything went wrong, before they even informed Ferguson of the aforesaid error.

Liam had decided upon two things while talking to Tommy. The first was that he should pay his friends a visit and see what, if anything, had occurred on their ends; and the second was that he would never set foot inside the Ginger Nightcap again.

The Young Ones

The three boys sat uncomfortably in Sparks bedroom; a world that was alien to all but Sparks, herself. A faux-oak Formica desktop sat inelegantly in the corner of the room, supported by twelve bottle crates of varying hues, six under either end, three high. This maladroit construction was in sharp contrast to the monster gaming computer that rested on top. The hard shell of the machine was as clear as glass, allowing Liam to see the inner workings in all their splendour; intermittently lit with green, red and blue flashing lights. Sparks had mentioned on a previous visit that the speed and length of the flashes allowed her to comprehend what was going on internally. Liam was not sure if he should believe that or not but it sounded cool.

On top of the desk and to the right of the computer were six, twenty-four-inch, 4K monitors. They were laid out, three-atop-three, all hanging on individual branches of their sturdy black steel stand. Above these monitors were three shelves, each housing a fifteen-and-a-half-inch laptop. Liam did not know much about computers or what they could do but he suspected that Sparks had put a lot of time and a serious amount of money into her setup. The monitors alone would have set her back a grand each, he supposed. How much she must have spent on the machine itself, Liam could not imagine.

On the walls of Spark's bedroom where you might ordinarily expect to find posters of young pop stars like Justin Bieber or film celebrities the likes of Johnny Depp, Sparks had sheets of coding lines; a life-size sketch of Einstein; and a photograph of Sparks shaking Larry Page firmly by the hand while Bill Gates photobombed from the sidelines.

On the day in question, Sparks sat upon her ergonomic, padded, black and red leather gaming chair while the three boys made themselves as comfortable as they could, enclosed together like caged game on Sparks single bed.

As it happened, 'caged game' would be a good metaphor for their current predicament. Each of them had, on the previous day, received a visit from Ferguson and his two goons and none of them were happy about it.

'I came in here,' Sparks announced, 'and they were at my computer. *My computer!* Do you understand how much of an invasion that is? How the hell he managed to get through the six passwords you need to get into it, I have no idea.'

'What was his name?' asked Liam. 'Was it Ron or Charlie?'

'Neither,' Sparks replied. 'This was another guy they called Snake. He's no looker but he can certainly code, I can tell you that.'

'They walked in when I was having my dinner,' Angus inserted. 'If my folks had been there, I'd have had a hard time explaining it to them. He ate my fish supper, too. Three chips he left me and *they* were all thin and hard.'

'Had a nice cosy chat did ye?' Shug piped in. 'Serves you right for running off on us, the other night. They got *me* in the bath, ya wee prick.'

'Look,' cried Angus, 'I said I was sorry. I panicked, okay? The polis' were right up next to me, closer than you two braggers, and I didn't have time to think. I just freaked out at the thought of going tae the jail and started running. I thought you guys would be right behind me.'

Shug gave him a shady look, 'Aye, sure you did.'

Liam was tired and stressed and the last thing he needed was bickering. 'Would you two shut up and listen fir a minute. We're in a bit of a bind here and I for one can't think of a way out of it. As far as I can tell, we have no choice but to do whatever Ferguson wants us to do and hope we get off lightly.'

Sparks sighed, unsure. 'And how likely do you think that is?'

'It's always possible,' Liam replied, unsure himself. 'I don't think there's any other option.'

'We could set your mum on him,' Angus suggested, nudging Shug as his face lit up in hilarity.

While Shug made a grab for Angus' nipples and the two friends rolled around on the bed, Liam and Sparks carried on from where they had left off, ignoring the carrying on beside them.

'I could maybe get into his computer,' Sparks thought out loud. 'It may be possible to find some damning information that we could use to barter our freedom.'

'Na,' said Liam, 'he'll only be working with hard copies. He's not the type to leave any sensitive information lying around like that. And imagine what he would do if he caught us. We'd be in even more shit than we are just now.'

Sparks massaged her temples with thumb and forefinger. 'Look, we can't do much of anything until we find out what it is that Ferguson actually wants. I'm sure it won't be too bad; nothing we can't deal with if we put our heads together. We are still kids, technically.'

Liam looked over at Angus and Shug as they fought beside him. 'I'd love to bang their heads together,' he said.

'You're not the only one,' Sparks assured him. 'I've often dreamed of giving each of them a right good kick up the arse.'

A broad smile crossed both faces in an all too brief moment of amusement, both knowing all too well that the days ahead of them were going to be far from jolly.

Butterflies in the Stomach

It was not long before Liam got a call from Ron, saying that Liam was attend The Keys, an exclusive restaurant and bar in the lusher part of town. The Keys differed from the Ginger Nightcap in almost every way. For instance, the Ginger Nightcap was a family tavern that sold the occasional microwaved pie, where everyone was welcome and were sure to be treated with as much respect as they proffered themselves. The Keys, on the other hand, was a high-end eatery which sold expensive cocktails; as opposed to the wide range of real ales and malt whiskies that the Ginger Nightcap offered. You would only be allowed admittance if they deemed you to be suitably dressed.

Liam was instructed to meet Ron there, the following evening, and made a point of telling Liam that he should have three hundred pounds on his person; cash. This small piece of information told Liam all that he needed to know. Being ordered to bring cash with him meant that he would not be expected to thieve anything but would instead be forced to sell drugs for the Ferguson family. The fact that the amount was three hundred pounds told Liam that it was going to be weed they were to take off of Ron's hands. An ounce of product to see how they did. If all went well, Liam knew that they would start to be trusted with more and more each time. Eventually, if appropriately trusted, they would be permitted a small amount on tick but that was a long way away and Liam hoped to all that was holy, they would no longer be involved in such activities by then.

But it was a mere dream, he knew it in his heart. Once wrapped up in that business, it became extremely difficult to get yourself out of it. Going straight was considered traitorous and was dealt with severely. They would much rather you were dead than free.

So, the four friends gathered all their disposable income and found that it came to just over the three hundred required. The remainder, it was decided, would be used for a taxi to and from The Keys.

Liam did not like the idea of walking up and down a street that the police would be sure to keep a close eye on. Many of the people who drank down that end of town were business executives or at least aiming to be in the next few years. Turning up in their Italian style, grey or black pinstriped suits; Burberry trench coats; and off-the-shelf Rolex watches, they came over from the city of Glasgow. Every weekend, they returned and were certainly the right type for The Keys. However, some had a tendency to get caught snorting cocaine in the cubicled facilities or get so completely wasted that they started to disregard such rules that were set in place by the establishment. This meant that many a middle-class yuppie would be tossed out onto the street with a grievance and no self-control when it came to speaking their mind. Therefore, the police made regular runs up and down, just in case some unlucky lads were stupid enough to start mouthing off to the locals who did not take kindly to disrespect and yobbery.

Ferguson was quite happy to welcome them in and sell them any amount of expensive drinks, up until just before an ambulance would be required. He was also an intelligent man and so made sure to eject anyone before they got to a point where his business would come under disrepute.

When Liam disembarked from the black cab, he stared at the window of The Keys and beyond. This was not his kind of place in the least. Why people paid twenty pounds a glass for a mix of spirits and fruit that they could make themselves at home for a couple of quid was more than Liam could comprehend. A one litre bottle of vodka came in at around fifteen pounds, Gin coming in at around the same price and you could get some cordials for about a pound a litre. With those and maybe some raspberries and small umbrellas, you could make yourself enough cocktails to cover you for the whole weekend; all for the low price of forty smackeroonies, as Liam liked to call it after hearing the comedian Kevin Bridges do the same. You would only get two drinks for that kind of money in Keys. Liam hoped that he did not have to buy any drinks while he was in there. He would be walking home, if he did.

Ambling through the etched glass doors that lead to the reception area, Liam, adorned in his usual blue jeans and black hoodie, begun to think he was a little underdressed for a place such as he was then frequenting. All the men there wore black or grey suits and shoes to match. Their shirts differed greatly, some with white and others in red, blue, purple or even pink. Liam could not understand why they felt that they needed to get dressed up just so they could go out on the piss *but*, he decided, *each to their own.*

As soon as Liam caught the receptionist's eye, she started to panic at the sight of such an uncouth person entering their elite establishment and instantly nodded to a security guard who made short work of nabbing Liam and dragging him off stage for a good talking to.

The sorry lad was dragged down a narrow corridor by his right ear, down some stairs and into a room that had less décor than a paper bag. There was furniture, it was true, but that furniture was two metal folding chairs and a table of the same suite. On the table, Liam saw a leather pouch which had been rolled up into a tubular package. A leather thong had been wrapped around it to keep it from unrolling again. This was not a room which Liam wanted to be in.

When the young lad was then pressed into one of the chairs and had his wrists cuffed to the arms of said chair, he quickly tried to explain that he was here on the request of Mr Ferguson to meet Big Ron.

He had been left alone at that point, as the overpaid security guard went away somewhere to locate Ron, carefully locking the door behind him. He was not sure if Liam was telling the truth or if he was just trying to wriggle out of trouble but he was not about to take any chances. He enjoyed a simple life and the last thing he needed was to upset such an employer as Willie Ferguson. It could go very bad for him, if he did.

As Liam waited in the dark and in silence, he thought on what a shit-show their transformation into teenage herbalists had already become; they had not even laid hands on the stuff, yet. If this were a glimpse into the future then Liam was not at all sure he could cope.

After what felt like an age, Liam heard a key in the lock and the door swung open again to reveal the handsy security guard, followed closely by the bulk that was Ron. His height was such that he had to bend slightly so as not to bump his head on the crossbeam. Ron smiled as he entered, seeing Liam trussed up as if he were a terrorist awaiting interrogation. All the time the security guard had been away, Liam found it difficult to take his eyes off of the leather wrap that lay on the metal table beside him. What was in it, he still did not know but he had a fair idea, judging by the obvious purpose of the room. Expressive interrogation was not on Liam's list of things he wanted to have done to him on that day and he was dreading what was to come next.

Liam looked Ron straight in the eye and said, 'Hey, I thought we were past all this. When you said you wanted me to come down here, I didn't think I was to be molested by this jumped up, wannabe watchman. He looks like he's just itching to start ripping out fingernails or something.'

'Aye, well if you wid come doon here looking like the last bastion o' beggerhood then whit dae ye expect?'

'I didn't expect to be hauled down here and tied to a chair for half an hour.'

'Only haulf an 'oor? Maybe we should leave off letting you out for a wee while longer, then. Is that what you want.'

It certainly was not. Liam hovered over the idea of a few curses and a bit of blasphemy but decided fairly quickly that this would not help his situation.

'Look,' Liam said, 'do you want me to do this business for you or will I just be on my way? I don't need this on top of everything else. You know full well that I didn't mean to upset Mr Ferguson in the first place.'

'Maybe not,' Ron replied, 'but upset him, ye did. 'Fit ye need tae dae, now is tae shut yer moo and listen tae fit we are wanting ye tae dae, if ye still want tae keep yer heed that is; and I'm no spikin' metaphorically, young loon.'

Liam managed to get the gist of what Ron had just told him and, wishing terribly to keep his head on top of his shoulders where it belonged, made the quick decision to stop talking and hear what Ron wanted to tell him.

Ron then nodded to the security guard who exited through the door once more, leaving the two of them alone in the small, cold room. Ron, denying Liam his freedom for a little longer, sat down in the opposite chair and stared the young boy down. 'Did ye bring yon cash wi ye?' he asked after a moment's deliberation.

Liam simply nodded, not looking to say anything that was not wholly necessary to the conversation at hand.

'Guid,' Ron continued. He stood up for a minute and walked over to Liam where he still sat, bound but ungagged. 'Fit pocket?' Ron asked.

Liam indicated that it was in his left jacket pocket and as Ron rummaged around and excavated the used notes, Liam thanked any god who was listening that he had not put the money in his trousers.

When Ron had retrieved the three hundred and odd pounds from Liam's pocket, counted it and slipped the the change back again[6], he pulled out a small package from his own jacket and dumped it onto Liam's lap.

'That's yers, noo. Get it sold and we can talk ag'in. This could be a wee bitty o' a money earner fir ye, so dinnae be mucking aboot and smoking it awe, yersel'.'

Liam chose not to make any remark that would upset Ron.

---

[6] Ron was a hardened gangster but he was no petty thief.

'Ye can sell yon ounce at fifteen quid a gram. That'll gie ye a profit o' a huner and twenty quid. Nae bad fir a couple o' night's work, eigh.'

Liam agreed that it was not too bad of a profit but he would certainly have to sell it by the gram. If he sold it in any larger amounts, he would be expected to drop the price exponentially. He did not foresee any issues with that, however. There were university and college students all over the place who were dying to get their hands on a decent smoke and Liam could clearly smell that the weed Ron had just dumped on his lap was indeed top-quality stuff. Liam may even determine later which strain it actually was but that was not a necessary piece of knowledge. Students were notoriously unfussy and would often be happy enough to buy anything, aromatically pungent or not, if they were having trouble getting it anywhere else.

Their business done, Liam asked as politely as he could muster, to be allowed out of the uncomfortable cuffs

'Unless ye wanna houf yon chair away with ye,' Ron suggested, smiling.

Liam smiled back, holding back the urge to punch Ron in his smug, self-satisfied face. What he wanted next was to get out of that room, away from the restaurant and into a taxi.

Upon finding himself home and clear, then and only then would he be able to relax and reflect on what to do next. He would, of course, call up the other three but that was a given. They would still have to figure out (a) how they were going to measure up the weed with none of them owning any scales; (b) what they were going to pack those grams into (little plastic bags was the most

94

usual but Liam certainly didn't keep such things lying about his mother's flat and he doubted any of the others had any, either); (c) where best to go that would give them the greatest chance of selling as much of the weed in one go as possible; and (d) what to do if they were caught.

These things would all have to be decided and soon. Liam felt the bag of weed burning a hole in his pocket. He wanted shot of it as soon as he possibly could. That would also mean that he would have to get another one from Ron but, Liam thought, he would cross that scary bridge when he came to it. For now, he just wanted to get home.

Ron indeed allowed him to leave of his own accord and on his own two feet. Liam did notice that, while making his way hurriedly through the front-of-house area, the receptionist gave the young scruff a look like she had just smelled something malodorous. The security guard merely gave him a look which said, *one day, son, you're all mine!*

Agony

The following morning, the four friends sat again in Spark's bedroom and stared at the open bag of weed. It was more than any of them had seen before and they spent a good while examining it and holding the larger buds up to their noses to get a good inbreath of what they considered to be the natural glory of God. It was astounding to all that they held in their inexperienced palms, an ounce of some of the most potent skunk in the city and were planning to sell it. If anyone had asked them previously if they ever thought they'd be experiencing the dingy underworld in this way, they would each have laughed heartily and claimed the speaker was being daft.

Now, however, they were in exactly that position and they needed to get it all sorted.

'So, how are we going to do this?' Liam asked as they admired their horde.

'We could use my mother's baking scales,' Sparks offered, 'but I don't think they weigh out to such a small amount as a single gram. I mean, when do you ever need but a gram of something when baking a cake?'

'Yeah, I don't think that would work,' Liam agreed.

'What about just doing it by eye?' Angus asked. 'It's not like any of them will have a set of scales on them to check and they'll probably tuck into it fairly smartly. They won't be able to tell if it's a bit out or not.'

'He's got a point,' Sparks agreed. 'College stoners aren't famed for their common sense.'

'I'm not sure,' wavered Liam.

It was at this point that Shug piped in. 'You're all being silly,' he stated, profusely. 'All you have to do is make up a set of pan scales out of whatever we can find lying around and weigh it out to the weight of a penny to give us three and a half gram bundles, then we just separate those up by eye. Not completely precise but more accurate in the long run.'

'How come you know how much a penny weighs?' asked Liam. 'Have you been smoking up the ganja and not telling the rest of us?'

'It's not like that,' Shug protested. 'My cousin is a stoner, through in Edinburgh, and he keeps giving me tips. He doesn't seem to realise I don't smoke as much as he does.'

'Well,' Sparks butted in, 'I suppose it was a good thing he did. Its looking like your idea is going to have to be what we do, if nothing else comes to mind?' She looked round at the others who shrugged. She turned her attention back to Shug. 'Fine, then. How is it that we go about making these pan scales you were talking about?'

And so, it occurred that they spend an hour piecing together all kinds of miscellaneous bits and bobs which Sparks had lying around her bedroom in order to build themselves a weighing machine. When it was all done. They sat back and looked it up and down, admiringly.

'Not too shabby, eh?' Liam suggested.

'Aye, it looks good, right enough,' Angus agreed.

The boys all turned their eyes on Sparks, the resident tech nerd. Realising that she was being watched and was expected to say something, Sparks looked at it once more before saying with a smile, 'Aye, that'll do, piggies, that'll do.'

They spent the next half hour weighing out all the grams and separating them from each other across the small lap tray which Sparks usually ate her dinner off of.

'So, what now?' Angus asked when they had completed their task.

'We need to find some small baggies to put them into,' Liam informed, 'though, I've no idea where we're likely to find twenty-eight tiny bags at this short a timescale.'

'I think I might be able to help, there,' Sparks suggested, chirpily, and dashed out of the room, knocking the tray in her excitement. She was mighty lucky that the weed was not thrown onto the floor in her excitement but it did mean that the boys had to start weighing the grams out all over again while Sparks ran off on her own small mission.

When Sparks returned from wherever she had ran off to, the boys were halfway through their repeated work.

'I've found some baggies,' Sparks announced as she came back into the room.

'How did you manage that?' Shug inquired. 'They're not exactly something people usually have hanging around the house, are they?'

'My sister makes her own earrings and the like,' Sparks explained. 'She uses these to package them.' She dumped them down on the tray, making the weed jump up and down on the spot.

'Will you watch what you're doing,' Shug demanded. 'I don't want to be starting from scratch, all over again.'

'But you're doing such a lovely job of it,' Sparks cooed.

'Bite me,' Shug replied, sulking.

Sparks grinned a secret wee grin to herself. *Not a bad idea*, she thought, eyeing him up and down.

Liam was looking quizzically at the small mounds of weed. 'We still need to figure out where we're going to sell this stuff,' he said.

'Wherever we do,' Shug warned, 'we'll have to make sure that we don't tread on any toes. There are probably dozens of small-time dealers in this area.'

'Then we'll go to Glasgow,' Angus suggested.

'It'll cost more than we'll earn back, if we all have to pay our bus fares etcetera,' Sparks downplayed.

'Then only one person goes,' replied Angus, upset that his idea wasn't being taken seriously.

'And where would this person go?' Liam asked, unsure if this was a good idea or a bad one. 'I don't think that walking the streets asking anyone if they're looking to score is the best way to get this done. Whoever goes will end up getting battered and having the whole lot, cash included, nicked off of them.'

'That's a fair point,' Shug agreed. 'We need to decide on a definite place to do it.'

'What about one of the student unions?' Sparks suggested.

'You need an I.D. to get in these days, I think,' sighed Liam. 'Otherwise, that would be perfect.

'How about,' Angus added, desperate to have his idea made real, 'if, whoever it is that goes, heads up to the union and tries to do a bit of scouting, outside. Find the ones most likely to partake in a little smoke and sort of get talking, let it slip that we can get our hands on what they need and see where that takes us.'

'Could do,' mulled Liam. 'Doesn't sound too scientific, though, does it?'

'If you want scientific, this isn't the business to be in,' said Shug.

'Well, this *is* the business we are in,' Liam replied. 'I just want to make sure that none of us are going to go down for this. You guys might be alright, first-time offence and all that, but I've had my two strikes. If I get caught dealing weed then I'm for the off. Straight to the jail; do not pass go, do not collect two hundred.'

'How about I go, then,' Angus thought out loud.

'Do you honestly think,' scorned Sparks, 'that we'd trust you to go off to Glasgow with an ounce of the finest skunk in your pocket and not have it go all horribly wrong?'

'I can do it, I promise,' pled Angus, rather downcast at the level of faith his friends had in him.

'I dunno,' Shug pondered. 'What do you think?' The last bit was directed at Liam.

Liam though it over for a minute, weighing not only the weed but the ups and downs of the suggested plan of action.'

He looked up at Angus, who was on the edge of his seat as he waited for the eventual verdict. 'Are you sure that you know what you're doing?' he asked the eager friend.

'Absolutely,' Angus assured.

'Okay then,' agreed Liam, slowly and to the protestations of Sparks and Shug. 'I would have preferred to sell it locally but I don't see how we can do that quickly, quietly and without stepping on any unfortunate toes.'

Angus grinned. 'It'll be fine,' he insisted. 'I'll get it sold quickly and be back on the last bus home.'

Sparks and Shug looked apprehensively at Liam. 'Are you sure this is a good idea?' asked Shug. 'I mean, he's my best friend and all that but you know yourself, he's not the brightest bulb on the shelf.'

'I'm sitting right here,' cried Angus. 'I *can* hear you, you know.'

'And you know it to be true, too,' Shug snapped. 'You're always making unfortunate decisions and getting the pair of us into fights and the like.'

'That won't happen,' Angus pledged. 'Whoever heard of a stoner getting themselves riled up enough to have a fight. One punch and they'd be down and not know why.'

'I think you're underestimating them,' Sparks disagreed. 'I know a few and they could all kick your arse and so could their girlfriends; no offence meant.'

'Oh,' Angus replied, in a sarcastic tone, 'none taken. What is this? Pick on the wee fella day?'

'I don't mean to be hard on you,' Sparks answered, 'but you do have a habit of getting into mischief. You could start a fight in an empty room.'

'Nothing will go wrong,' Angus implored. 'I can do this.'

'Fine, then,' Liam eventually agreed. 'The weed's all paid for, so if we lose the lot then at least we won't be under the boot of Ferguson for it. It'll just mean that we will have to find another three hundred quid to pay for the next ounce. Off you go, then and if you don't come back, we'll assume you're in the cells.'

'Fair enough,' Angus replied as he took the long brown envelope containing the twenty-eight smaller packages, along with the rest of the money they had scrammed up.'

'I'll just say one more thing before you go,' Shug said, as Angus was putting on his coat.

'What's that?' Angus asked.

Shug put a comforting hand on the boy's shoulder. 'Don't fuck this up!' he said.

*

The day passed and then so did the evening. When two of the am came and went, Liam, Sparks and Shug were starting to get very nervous indeed. Angus had promised to be home on the last bus. However, the X77, which went through Loganswell and Fenwick, left West Campbell Street in Glasgow at just before ten-past-ten and arrived in Kilmarnock at twenty-to-eleven. There was no way on earth that it could take anywhere near that long to get from where the driver would have thrown

109

him off the bus and find his way up to Sparks' house, even if he stopped off at home for some reason.

They had tried calling his mobile many times. The first few times it rang out without Angus answering it. The other ten times, it had gone straight to voicemail. The concern of the three friends grew and grew and none of them knew what on earth they were supposed to do. They had known what Angus was like and, indeed, they had voiced their worries about letting him go off on that highly important mission. But let him go they had. They were since regretting allowing him to persuade them that he could complete the task at hand without a massive cockup.

A massive cockup is indeed what they suspected when four o'clock came round the corner.

'He'll have either got himself mugged or arrested,' Shug said, solemnly. 'It's always one or the other with him.'

'How many times has he been arrested, now?' Liam asked.

'Oh, must be about ten or eleven at the last count,' Shug considered.

'Then why,' Sparks asked, 'has he never been charged for anything. Has he the luck of the Irish or something? Been kissing the Blarney stone?'

'One of his uncles is a top-shot solicitor in the city,' Shug informed the other two. 'The wee tit's not long in the cells before he's back out on the street again, always with no charges being brought. If he is ever charged, they're aye quashed before it even goes to trial. No trial means nothing on his record. Free and clear with no black marks. Lucky bastard.'

'He is indeed,' Liam agreed, thinking on his own black marks. 'But I'm still worried about what has happened to him. What if he's lying in some Glaswegian street, unconscious and bleeding?'

'Glaswegians are good folk,' Sparks said, softly. 'If anything's happened to him then someone will at least pack him off to the nearest hospital; the Royal Infirmary is the closest, I checked just after he left. It's not like Edinburgh where they're more likely to ignore some poor soul lying incapable on the street.'

'That doesn't really help with my concerns,' replied Liam. 'I just hope he's alright. It's worse because there's nothing we can do from here and going into Glasgow would be pointless; he could be anywhere.'

'He'll be fine,' Shug cooed. 'He'll turn up eventually. He always does.'

'That is true,' Sparks agreed. 'Remember that time,' she recalled, 'when we went up to that Rock Ness concert in the highlands?' The two boys nodded. 'Well, he vanished on the first night there and we didn't see him again till we got back down here and found him in the pub, drinking with some girl he had met up north and brought down here in order to *'show her around'*.'

'She was a wee stunner, that one,' Shug mused. 'A few cups knocked over in the top closet, if you know what I mean, but you can't have everything.'

Really, Sparks thought. *Is that a fact?*

'Women are like cars,' Liam mused, 'it's all very well having big headlights but if there's nothing under the hood then it's not going to work.'

Sparks scowled at Liam, feeling that she should be offended by his comment but couldn't fault the logic. She was well in favour of the importance of brains over breasts.

'There was one time,' Shug continued, 'that he actually managed to disappear from us while we were on a class trip to Newcastle. He turned up again, five minutes before we were about to get on the hired bus which was to take us back home again. He still hasn't told me what he got up to down there. There's a lot we don't know about that one; always keeps his cards close to his chest.'

'I know,' said Liam, 'Having a friend like that can be tough. It's like having blackouts, when you don't know where they go or what they do after they've left your sight.'

'Well,' Shug pressed on, 'my point still stands. He's probably holed up somewhere having the time of his life.'

'Yeah,' Sparks concurred, 'but he's doing it with our weed and/or our money; depending on whether he's sold it or not.'

'You don't think he's pissing it all away, do you?' asked Liam, concerned.

Sparks looked shocked.

'Na,' Shug assured them. 'He's one of these folk who can find a swimming pool in the desert. He'll have found a way to have his fill without shifting a penny.'

'He'd better do,' Liam scowled, 'or he's in for a nasty shock when I get my hands on him.'

It was then that they all went silent, their ears swiftly directed at the bedroom door. A creaking sound could be heard, alike to someone failing to walk softly across the upstairs corridor floor.

'I thought your parents were away off to the coast for the weekend?' Liam inquired in a soft whisper.

'They are,' Sparks mouthed back, 'and my sister has set herself up at her boyfriend's house while they're away. There shouldn't be anyone but us three in the house.'

They all stared at the door as the creaking came ever closer before coming to a sudden stop. It was then that the door started to slowly creep open. When it had fully opened and a shadowy figure was revealed, Sparks picked up threw the nearest thing to hand, which happened to be a pair of Presch punch pliers which Sparks used for putting holes in leather; belts and watches mostly. She was a multi-capable girl.

Angus screamed as the hole punch cracked him on the head.

'What'd you do that for?' he asked, almost through tears. 'That really hurt.'

'Where the hell have you been, you little tit,' Sparks yelled. 'We've been worried sick. Thought you might have been lying dead in a ditch or something, stripped of all but your boxers.'

'Don't wear boxers,' Angus grinned. 'Commando's the only way to go; so refreshing.'

Sparks was momentarily derailed. 'That's disgusting,' she managed before remembering what she was at. A stapler flew through the air after the hole punch.

Angus screamed again. 'Will you stop doing that?' he begged. He looked to the others for some help. 'Guys? Tell her to stop throwing things at me.'

'She's not wrong,' Liam replied. 'You were supposed to be back here by eleven at the latest. We didn't know what had come of you. And then you come in here as if nothing was wrong. What's wrong with your head?'

'It's had a couple of knocks,' Angus sobbed, staring at Sparks like a smacked puppy who doesn't understand what it did wrong, 'that's what's happened to it.'

'Look,' Shug interjected, 'why don't you start by telling us if you managed to get the weed sold or not.'

Angus looked offended. 'Of course, I did. Told you I would and that's what went down. Made a pretty profit, too.'

'What do you mean?' Sparks inquired, suspiciously.

'What I mean is,' Angus continued, obviously still upset at being near knocked out twice in as many minutes, 'is that I managed to make us a butt load more than the hundred and twenty profit.'

'How did you do that?' Liam asked. 'Did you put the price up or something?'

'To start with,' Angus answered, smiling happily again as he recalled his evening. 'Sold the lot for twenty quid a gram. Never saw me coming the wastrels.'

'So that's a two-hundred-and-sixty-pound profit,' Sparks calculated.

'Nope,' Angus corrected, 'a bit more than that.'

'How,' Shug queried.

'Well,' Angus went on, 'I nabbed some of them back when they weren't looking then sold it to them again when they couldn't find the culprit.'

'But that culprit was you,' Liam pointed out.

'Certainly, it was but *they* didn't know that.' Angus beamed from ear to ear.

'So how much profit did you really make, then?' asked Liam, curiously baffled at this exchange.

'Five hundred,' Angus announced.

'Five hundred,' the other three all shouted at the same time.

'Yup,' confirmed Angus. 'I sold twelve back to them at the same price; twenty a gram.'

Liam, Shug and Sparks all stared at Angus as if they were seeing some holy incarnation; or the devil himself. They couldn't truthfully decide which.

'Well, minus the bus fare..' Liam started before he was interrupted.

'Nope. Didn't cost me a penny,' Angus informed him. 'I told the driver that my old mum had been taken into the hospital and they wouldn't allow me to ride in the ambulance with them and if I didn't get to the Royal this very night, I may never get the chance to see her again. A few tears and some jibber-jabber and he let me ride for free.'

The others were greatly shocked to hear that their friend would stoup to such lengths to avoid paying the fare for a thirty-minute bus ride.

'And on the way back, I managed to hop a ride with Ginger Henry who had been in town to visit his big brother. We ended up meeting at the same house party and came home together in his grandad's old Morris Minor. You know, the nineteen-fifty-eight Cabriolet? Beautiful machine.' He started to drift off somewhere in the memory of it.

'What about your phone, then?' Shug asked, still in shock from Angus' tale. 'We tried to call you multiple times and you never answered. It eventually started sending us straight to voicemail.'

Angus actually looked a little guilty at this point. 'My little sister got hold of my phone this morning and changed the ringtone to some Dua Lipa song and I didn't realise till I was on the bus. Bloody thing went off as we were passing the Pollock Park. Didn't realise it was mine, at first. I didn't have time to go changing it by then, so I stuck it on silent. Didn't know then that I'd also switched off the vibration. When I did pull out my phone to call you, it was dead from all your ruddy phone calls. No charger and no place to plug it in, even if I did happen to be carrying one. Just had to make my way home and hope you were still up.'

'There's a point,' Sparks quizzed. 'How did you manage to get into my house? I know I definitely locked all the doors after you left.'

'You did, for sure,' Angus approved, 'but you missed the downstairs bathroom window.'

There's no bathroom downstairs,' Sparks started. 'Wait, do you mean the bog? You managed to fit that fat arse through the toilet window? It's tiny.'

'Not the first time and probably won't be the last,' chortled Angus.

A mug bearing the face of the Lord Byron's daughter, Ada Lovelace, the world's first computer programmer, hit Angus in the same spot as the punch and stapler had.'

Angus started crying. 'Stop it,' he sobbed, through all-to-real tears. 'How would you like it if I started throwing things at you?'

'Try it and see how your face looks afterwards,' Sparks retorted. 'All you've had so far have been taster samples, compared to what I'd do to you, if you lay a hand on me.'

Angus gave a whimper but was at least smart enough to know when to keep his mouth shut.

Liam, who had been staring at the eight hundred pounds Angus had passed him. 'Well, I guess I'll have to go and see Ron again,' he whined, 'but we have to make sure that from now on we serve our customers well, if we're to make a proper go of this.' Angus begun to make a comment. 'Yes, Angus, you've done well, nobody's denying that but if we are to deal with those guys again, excuse the pun, then we can't go cheating them anymore or they'll figure out what's happening and then you will be in a pile of shit; not only from them but from Ferguson's boys, too. We need to do this properly.'

The others all agreed and Liam pocketed the three hundred pounds that was to go to Ron. They then spit up the other five hundred between them, before ordering themselves a late-night chippy from the only place in town to be open through the night.

Even with their newly found troubles, obstacles and dilemmas, they were managing to get through the mess which they had unwittingly gotten themselves into. Maybe, just maybe, they would find a way to make this all work without the whole thing going to shit.

No Problem

Five and a half months went by and everything seemed to be going well. The four friends had managed to make the best of their bad situation and, all-in-all had failed to have any incidents that could not quickly be resolved. They were in a good place, mentally, and they were even, it seemed, to be enjoying a good working relationship with Ron and Charlie whom they had met each and every week since their initiation into the brotherhood, as it were. It turned out that Ron and Charlie had both been policemen in a previous life but, having become disenfranchised with the lack of funding and low pay, they had allowed Ferguson to get his hands on them and eventually they were part of the family; rising stars in the business.

Ron had told them that, with the money he was earning under Ferguson, he would be able to retire twenty years before he would have been able to, if he had stayed in the force. This idea definitely appealed to the four friends. None of them were very interested in traditional careers anyway and this thought was somewhat comforting. It was nice to hear someone in the business speak of possible retirement, allowing them the belief that retirement was indeed possible, after all. Up until that point, they had all believed and maybe still did, that getting out, as they say, was a near impossibility that only came to the fortunate few who managed to hold on to some kind of evidence against their rogue of an employer. Liam couldn't see them getting to the same level of trust as Ron and Charlie received but, still, it was a reassuring thought to think that, one day, this all might just be over. If the four friends ever did get on Ferguson's nerves then their future would involve a night-time sea voyage and a pair of concrete wellies.

Nevertheless, even though all seemed to be going well with the business, Liam's home life had become quite stressful. In the time that they had spent moving weed for Ferguson, Liam's mother had become more ill than before. She had been taken to the hospital and been kept in on a permanent basis. She was now spending all of her time in bed, unable to move any more than it took to turn herself over and onto her side and the doctors had told Liam that there was nothing more that could be done for her but to make her comfortable.

The time would come very soon when they would have to consider next steps. Liam knew exactly what they meant but there was no way on God's green earth that he would go down that road until it was absolutely necessary. If it came to it, he did not even know for sure if he would be able to make that decision or not.

One thing he was adamant about was that he would never allow his father to be the one to make any judgments on his mother's health or what to do next. He had been out of their lives for many years and Liam saw no need for him to get involved now, once things had really started to go bad for them. His father was not about to abruptly sweep in and play at being head of the household, again. Liam would make sure of that.

It tore Liam up to think of it but, if the time came when she was in more pain than she should ever have to bear and it became clear that she was at her end, then he would have to do right by his mother and make the terrible decision. Liam cried inside every time he saw her, lying there, in her hospital bed. She was tied to so many machines, Liam could not remember the names of any of them. All he knew was that there was one that did the job of her lungs; one that he guessed was probably termed a feeding tube; one that was attached to her left arm by way of injected needles and clear tubing where her blood could be seen all too visibly; and they had attached some sort of pulse generator to her chest in case her heart stopped and the nurses had to step in quickly to get it going again. She even had a catheter because of her inability to get out of the bed or even communicate to the nurses that she needed to go.

Basically, Liam's mother did not have long left in the world and it was a constant worry to the young boy. Thankfully, he was soon to be sixteen and the social would not have to get involved. He would, however, have to find some way of paying the rent, etcetera. Liam shivered as the thought appeared. *He would have to get a job.*

As Liam walked into the Keys, he scratched at his neck where the shirt collar was rubbing. He had been gifted, out of necessity, a new Hart Schaffner Marx, New York style, Solid Stretch Wool Suit with a Harris Tweed waistcoat. The boss had even thought it prudent to include three shirts and three ties; a pair of very distinguished shoes; and, for some bizarre reason, a set of sock braces (Liam could not bring himself to refer to them as suspenders). They looked like the braces which people would normally use to keep their trousers from falling down around their ankles, but quite a bit smaller.

This had all been a necessary step in Liam's rise to appearing respectable. People had obviously complained about the wee neddy who kept brazenly walking into

131

reception in clothes that were simply not suitable for the clientele's eyes. Ferguson must have thought the best plan all round was to smarten Liam up a bit. So that was what they had done. Liam couldn't be sure, of course, that this was how it all went down. All he knew about it was that, on one of his weekly visits to the Keys, Ron had given the boy a package that he said was from Mr Ferguson; *as a wee thank you.* Liam was told to make sure he wore it at all times when conducting business for Ferguson and especially when he was attending Keys.

Which is why, as Liam entered the Keys for the seventh time since he began working for Ferguson, he actually appeared like he belonged. The suit gave Liam an air of credibility and this young, small-town ned, dressed in Laird's clothing, caught the eye of many a female guest.

On entering, Liam went straight to reception. The girl on the desk, who had been on duty every time he had visited before, failed to recognise him.

'I have a meeting with Ronald Gove,' Liam informed her.

'And who shall I say has arrived?' she asked, politely and with a smile he had never thought she could possess.

'Leopold Fionnlagh Macrae,' he stated.

The girl diligently wrote this down before looking slightly puzzled. She looked up again and studied Liam's recently washed face, which sat underneath his coconut scented, fair coloured hair. 'Oh,' she stated, coldly, as she slipped into the vernacular, 'it's you, int'it?' She sighed. 'Wait here while I get him.' Before leaving, she looked Liam up and down once more, unable to believe that such a transformation was possible.

When the receptionist returned, she was followed by both Ron and Charlie. Liam had never seen them both at the same time before; not since their first meeting. He suspected, therefore, that seeing them together was because they all wanted to gawp at the pleb who had metamorphosed into a right little gentleman. It was all Liam could do not to call them out on it. Instead, he managed to bite his lip and stay silent as they gawped at him, grinning like a hippy who was in a particularly good mood.

Eventually, their amusement passed and the receptionist went back to her work. Charlie left by the front doors, telling Ron that he would see him later that night, '...*for that thing, at the place.*'

Liam had no idea what that was referring to but he suspected that they were up to no good.

When they were alone, Ron took Liam through to another, more private room. This room was a lot nicer than the first one he had seen. It had fancy wallpaper; beautiful redwood armchairs, upholstered in brown leather and brass studs; and the walls were lined with old portraits in great, thick frames. All amassed together, it gave Liam a sense of old men in suits, smoking and drinking brandy. The massive coal fire on one side of the room brought this vision into full effect.

It was here that the two proceeded to work through their usual routine where Liam would pass Ron his three hundred pounds and Ron would pass Liam a brown package, carefully wiping off any of his fingerprints that might have been left there. This done, Liam made to leave but was stopped at the last moment by Ron who said, 'Oh, wan mair 'hing. Mr Ferguson wuid like a word.'

'What? Now?' Liam asked, concerned.

'Naw, ya wee numpty,' Ron growled. 'Fit wye wid he be wantin' tae be onywhere near ye, wi that stuff honking up the joint? Use yer heid, loon.'

It had taken Liam some time to get a grip of Ron's inimitable blend of Doric and Glaswegian but he thought he was starting to get the hang of it. He would never attempt to speak it in Ron's presence but that isn't to say that he was not at home each night, practicing in front of the mirror.

'When, then?' Liam asked.

'The morrow night,' Ron replied. 'Be here at seven and be sure tae huv yon suit on when ye arrive; y'll be huvin' dinner wi him.'

Liam thought this a terrible idea. His throat dried up immediately on hearing the words come out of Ron's mouth and he went

136

like stone, unable to move, with his brain desperately trying to process this information.

'I can't...' Liam cried as he finally managed to get his brain to reach his mouth, 'I can't be having dinner with the likes of Mr Ferguson, not in his own restaurant. I'm just a nobody. Why would he want me there? I'll just end up dirtying the noses of everyone there. They'll all just know that I'm not one of them; an imposter.'

'Look here,' Ron growled again. 'I'm only going to tell ye this wance and if you tell onyone, I'll deny it whole-heartedly.' He leaned into Liam, conspiratorially. 'Ye're just as guid as ony o' those posh pricks, through there. Ne'er forget that. They may huv mair money than sense but you've got brains and skills that they'll ne'er huv.' Ron stood up straight again. 'You're also the only wan that Mr Ferguson wants at his dinner table, the morrow evening. That's a big 'hing and that's why they'll hate you.'

Liam did not know what to think about that.

'So,' Ron concluded, 'you ken fit tae dae?'

'What?' asked Liam.

'Ignore them aw. They dinnae matter a jot and ye will be the maist important wan in the room. Act like it. Mak' yon room yer own and ne'er let onyone talk doon tae ye; *unless it's me, Charlie or Mr Ferguson, o' course.* You dae huv tae mind yer place, after a'.'

'I'll remember,' Liam replied, 'and thank you. I appreciate the candour.'

'Dinnae fret, loon,' Ron replied. 'I huv yer back, e'en when ye dinnae ken it.'

'Appreciated,' was all that the shocked Liam could get out.

'Right,' Ron went on, as he left the room. 'Mind and be here at six forty-five, sharp.

You dinnae want to be keepin' him waitin' noo, dae ye?'

'Of course,' Liam answered, shaking a little.

Ron turned, once more before leaving. 'An' mind, loon, act the prince in front o' abody an' they'll treat ye like wan.'

Liam was not sure about this but promised that he would do his best. Man and boy then parted ways, allowing Liam to pop home and change into some more comfortable clothes before the others were due to visit. Liam's mum's house had become the metacentre for their operation. With his mother in the hospital for the foreseeable future, this allowed Liam, Sparks and the other two to utilise his mother's kitchen to measure and bag up.

They had bought themselves a specific set of electronic scales with the first five hundred pounds they had earned. The scales themselves only cost a couple of hundred but while they were in Glasgow, they decided to have a slap-up dinner and a night on the town to celebrate. It was a nice break from the norm and they all had a most enjoyable day. Angus even managed to get there and back without disappearing off somewhere. Life had felt good.

The Good Life

The next evening, Liam arrived at the Keys restaurant ahead of time and so hovered in the comforting shadows of a shop doorway across the street. He stayed there for ten minutes, collar up to keep away the evening's cooling air, as he puffed on a cigarette and geared himself up for the even more uncomfortable evening ahead of him.

As he inhaled and exhaled in recurring succession, all the ways he could ruin the evening scrolled past his mind's eyes. There were many. Some were more probable than others but he made a promise to himself to avoid each and every one. Liam needed that evening to go as smoothly as possible. Therefore, with his heart beating a rondo in his chest, *ABACABA, ABACABA, ABACABA...*) and sweat rapidly forming all about his anxious frame, he sought to consider happier thoughts.

The fact that Ron considered him to be a better person than most of the clientele behind those exterior glass walls gave him a little hope but not much. He was terrified but adamant that he was going to see it through. *I can do this*, he kept reiterating as he allowed himself to take charge of his quickening breaths. *In through the nose. Out through the mouth.* Slowly, his hurried breathing soothed and he relaxed, enabling his heart rate to slow, once again. *I can do this.*

Geared up, Liam pinged his cigarette stub onto the street where the prodigious street sweeper would take care of it the next morning and stepped off of the pavement, his lips forming a silent mantra to calm his nerves.

As soon as he entered the reception area, Liam was bundled into the restaurant and placed at a table, specially reserved for the evening's delights. Placed in prime position, the table was close enough to the bar so they would not have any trouble ordering drinks and far enough away from the toilets to ensure they were never bothered by people barging past them.

As Liam sat there, awaiting Mr Ferguson's arrival, he sipped on his lemon flavoured tonic water. Looking around the room, he noticed a few faces turn his way before snapping back to their companions when they caught Liam's inquisitive gaze. He found himself praying that Ferguson would fail to show and Liam could scurry on home again.

The atmosphere made him feel like a monkey in the clothes of a prince, well dressed but certainly not something most people would wish at their dinner table. All his life he had kept to the shadows, never allowing himself to be noticed, and now he was about to have dinner in the most exclusive restaurant in town with a man who was considered to be one of the baddest gangsters around. There were only a few people around Kilmarnock who weren't deathly afraid of the old gangster and Liam did not count himself among them. Liam shook to his boots whenever his name was mentioned and the last thing the young boy wished to do was upset him.

Thinking again about deep waters and concrete wellies, he shuddered and downed his drink to tame his rapidly acquiring cotton mouth, before waving the glass ceremoniously at the barman.

Another was quickly issued. This was just in time. Ferguson walked into the room just as Liam was taking the first sip.

Liam breathed in and out as deep and as slow as he could manage. He was determined that the dinner should go well and he was going to make sure he was on his best behaviour.

'Young Mr Macrae,' Ferguson greeted as he reached the table,' I am glad you found the time for us to enjoy this meal together. We haven't seen much of each other in a while and I thought it would be nice to spend a little time together and catch up.'

'It's appreciated,' Liam replied, standing up and respectfully shaking the man's hand.

'Please,' Ferguson continued, once Liam's moist palm left his grip, 'have a seat. Have you had a chance to look over the menu yet?'

'I'm afraid not,' said Liam. 'I'm not sure I would know what any of it was, even if I had.' He tried to smile at Ferguson, who returned it.

'How about I just order for the two of us, then. I'm sure we can find something to your liking.'

Liam nodded, gratefully and Ferguson called over the head waiter as another placed a large whisky in front of him. 'My guest will take a double Black Macallan M., straight away. He can't be drinking tonics all night.' The waiter, passing the underage boy a glance that reeked of disapproval, gestured to the barman and the whisky, at over two hundred and forty pounds a glass, was retrieved from its perch and dusted off.

Ferguson perused the menu as they waited for the staff to bring out the drinks, table breads and jug of water. The head waiter then returned and laid a glass, containing two perfect spheres of ice, and a smaller jug of water on the table before the young lad.

Ferguson addressed the waiter again who instantly pulled a pad and pen from out of his apron. 'I think we'll start off with the Foie Gras de Canard;' he said, 'then, I believe the Oysters in White Truffle Sauce would go down delightfully; and for mains? I am just burning to try the 12oz Tajima Wagyu Ribeye with Sauce Diane. It's supposed to be divine.' The waiter dutifully wrote this all down. 'Also,' Ferguson continued, 'we'll reserve our desserts now. Put aside two of the Saffron Cheesecakes with Grated Sekai Ichi Apples.'

'Any wine for the table, sir?' the waiter inquired.

'Indeed,' Ferguson cooed. 'I think we'll have the Domaine, Ramonet Montrachet, Grand Cru for the starter; and, let me see, yes. Let us have a bottle of the 1945

Chateau Margaux; the Vandermeulen, if you please.

The waiter wrote this all down and scurried off, first to the dessert cart, in order to ensure that there were indeed still two cheesecakes left and, if there were, to set them aside safely from the rest.

A couple of minutes later, the first bottle of wine was brought to them. The waiter, holding the bottle in a white cloth napkin, uncorked it in front of them and poured a little into Ferguson's glass. Ferguson swirled the small amount around the sides of his glass, before raising it to his nose and having a sniff. It was not until then that he eventually placed it to his lips and began to drink; though only a sip. To Liam's surprise, he then started making short sharp but repetitive kissing noises. Liam had never seen anything like it but nobody else in the room seemed to find this ritual out of the ordinary, so he guessed that it was the thing to do.

Ferguson seemed happy enough. After he had completed his routine, he placed the glass back on the table, nodded to the waiter and turned his attentions back to Liam. The waiter filled both their glasses, dropped the wine into an ice bucket and left, quick-sharp.

It was then that Ferguson, reneging on his patient observance of Liam, chose to speak.

'So,' he said, completely relaxed and at ease, 'tell me a bit about yourself. Family? Hobbies? That sort of thing.'

This was the kind of question Liam hated. He did not think his life was all that interesting and he struggled to think of anything to tell Ferguson, that he would be interested to hear.

'There's not much for the knowing,' Liam replied as genteel as he dared. 'I grew up round here. Mum's sick and Dad's out of the picture. I don't really have any hobbies to speak of.'

Ferguson looked at him and smiled, pleasantly. 'You certainly have an eventful homelife,' he said. 'If there is ever anything a humble man like myself can do to ease the strain, please let me know.'

'That's appreciated, Mr Ferguson,' Liam acknowledged, 'but I think we're about maxed out on miracles.'

'Very well,' Ferguson replied. 'Do drink the wine, it's a cheeky little number.'

Liam did not know how a glass of wine could give someone cheek but he did not question it. Instead, he placed the glass to his lips and downed half the glass. He then put the glass back onto the table and wiped his mouth with the back of his hand.

The whole room gasped.

Liam almost had a heart attack, the moment he realised what he had just done. He had tried his best to make his apologies to Ferguson, who simply laughed and told him, 'Don't worry, son. I have done worse than that myself, before now. Please, do continue.'

Liam looked back down at the glass, guiltily. 'It is very nice, Mr Ferguson,' He said. 'I might get some for my mother. A spot of wine won't make her any worse.'

'A single bottle comes in at around nine hundred and forty-five pounds. In here, it would come in at around sixteen hundred.'

Liam, who had been taking a sip at the time, almost spat a mouthful all over the table. He miraculously succeeded in keeping it in and swallowed hard. 'Sixteen hundred pounds?' he asked in astonishment.

'Indeed,' replied Ferguson, 'don't even ask about the red.'

Liam swallowed again, this time out of shock. 'I usually get mum's wine down at the supermarket; seven-ninety-nine a bottle. Nothing that tasted as good as this.'

'Well, tonight we are able to enjoy the finer things in life,' Ferguson proclaimed. 'Life is for the living, young Mr Macrae, and what use is having money, if you don't spend it?'

Liam saw some logic in this.

For the rest of the meal, man and boy discussed more generic topics and generally had a nice time. Liam was nervous all the way through, still unaware why Ferguson had wished to have dinner with him, in the first place. The meal, however, was incredible. He had never enjoyed a meal so much, and there was a great deal of it. Liam filled his boots and then some, until he could not eat another thing. Thankfully, he had managed to consume the cheesecake before this happened. It was as delicate as anything Liam had ever tasted before and melted in the mouth so softly that he barely felt it touch his tongue.

All that being said, Liam was enjoying his evening; even in the knowledge that he was in the company of a ruthless gangster who appeared to be playing the part of a hospitable host. Liam wondered how long he was going to keep it up. *Where's the catch?* Liam asked himself, in the quiet of his own head.

Once Liam had eaten as much as he could without rupture, he dropped his napkin onto his plate, just as he had seen Ferguson do, ten minutes previously. He looked at Ferguson, who had been studying him all that time.

'Sorry it took me so long,' Liam apologised.

'Not at all, son,' Ferguson replied, earnestly. 'I have not enjoyed a meal as much as this one in a long time. Maybe we shall be able to do it again, some time.' He left this hanging.

Liam, who knew when his cue had arrived, said, 'Of course, Mr Ferguson. It would be an honour.'

'Good, good,' Ferguson replied and ordered a bottle of something called a Sticky Mickey. Liam was informed that it was a dessert wine, made from French grapes but it was all like Greek to the young lad. He had trouble telling a raisin from a sultana. The knowledge of which grape was which, well, that was a complete mystery to him.

It tasted sweet and Liam found that he actually liked it. The wines had been good, of course, but they were not really anything that he would go out and buy for himself, even if he could afford it. This orangey-yellow liquid was more to his tastes. It tasted like a melon, or maybe mango; he could not tell which. On the tongue, however, there seemed to be a lingering limey tang.

'Is it to your satisfaction,' Ferguson asked, politely.

'It is, Indeed,' Liam answered, gratefully.

'I shall have them give you a half-bottle to take home with you. I'm afraid they don't come in any larger quantities than that.'

'That would be lovely, Mr Ferguson, but you don't have to do that.'

'Not a problem, my boy,' Ferguson chided. 'It is nowhere near as expensive as the other bottles you just drank, so don't worry, please. I simply prefer it over the more expensive ones. Always remember, cost doesn't always mean quality.'

Liam didn't worry at all. In his full belly and his vinery delights, he was more than palatable.

This was the point that Ferguson chose to change the subject.

'I suppose you've been speculating as to why I invited you to diner, this evening,' he postulated.

'I had wondered,' Liam admitted.

'I have a proposition for you,' he said, slowly.

This is it, Liam thought. *This is where we discover the rub.*

Ferguson folded his napkin and laid on the table where his dessert used to reside, situating his glass on top. 'I have heard word about three vehicles, leaving a certain site this coming weekend. The person receiving the delivery is not one whom I would consider a friend; quite the contrary, in fact.'

'That's fair enough,' Liam belched, before slouching down in his chair, in embarrassment.

'Quite,' Ferguson acknowledged. 'What I propose is that you and your three associates requisition them for me.'

This made Liam sit up and pay attention. 'You want us to nick some posh cars?' he asked, unbelievingly. He went down to a whisper. 'We've never really done it properly, before. We only took, you know, *yours*, as a laugh. Before we knew who they belonged to, of course.' He held up his hands in portrayed naivety.

'Indeed,' scowled Ferguson, 'but now is the time, you join the big boys. You have been doing sterling work, I am told, and I believe that you are ready for a new challenge.'

'I'm not sure...' Liam tried but Ferguson was not taking the hint.

'You will do fine, Mr Macrae. I would put it in the hands of no other.'

Liam squirmed. He did not feel able to refuse Ferguson and he had eaten too much to allow him the option of running away. He was in a bind and so, downcast and praying desperately, he agreed.

Their business completed, Ferguson's jovial persona returned and they enjoyed, for the most part, the rest of their dessert wine. Afterwards, they had a glass of Tawney Port before retiring. Liam returned home, more than a little drunk, and Ferguson proceeded wherever he went of an evening. Liam did not wish to even imagine what he could be getting up to.

One thing that Liam did take away from the evening was one of the menus. He wished dearly to show the others what he had been eating while he had been appropriating the sweet life for a few hours.

He had enjoyed almost every minute of it. Now, however, he had to go back home and tell the others that they were being promoted from weed dealers all the way up to car thieves.

Before he had left, Liam had been slipped a package by the snooty receptionist. Unknown to Liam at the time it contained photographs of the cars, where they would be held, a map of the area and a small dossier which explained everything they would be expected to know.

He certainly thinks ahead, Liam mused.

Duty Free

Back in Liam's mum's flat, they sat around the kitchen table and opened the package together. Ferguson had given a brief talk on what was to be done. What he had not been was clear on was any actual detail. Therefore, when they opened up the package and found, underneath the layers of brown paper, the plans for a transport ship, they were all taken aback.

'This can't be right,' Sparks commented, never having expected such a location for the cars to be.

'I guess it must be,' replied Liam, laying out the map and the photographs of the cars, before opening the dossier. He read the dossier. 'Aye, it is, right enough,' he continued after perusing the printed sheets. 'It says here that the current owner is planning to transport them out of the country in around three days' time. They're being stored on the ship until then. We've got to find a way to get the cars off of the ship and back to this warehouse,' he indicated it on the map, 'before our window closes and the ship sails away with the score.'

'Why us?' asked Shug. 'We're just a bunch of plebs. What do we know about nicking high-end cars? We're going to die, aren't we?'

'I said the same thing to Ferguson,' Liam replied. 'He wasn't having any of it; says we've impressed him and he wants to give us, what he calls, a promotion. I assume its because we're expendable.'

'Oh, great,' Angus piped in, 'the last thing we wanted was to get in further with this maniac and his mates. What're we gonna do?'

'We're going to look over the job,' Liam reassured, 'and we're going to see if there is any way we can reasonably get it done.'

'And what if we can't?' Shug inquired.

'Then we're in a lot of shit and will probably have to run for our lives from this town. I'm thinking about up north, somewhere. The west coast, maybe. What do you think?' This last bit was directed at Sparks who had been perusing all the documents and the map while the agitated exchange had been going on.

Sparks looked up. 'What?' she asked, absentmindedly.

'I was asking you what you thought of our chances?' Liam repeated.

'Oh, well,' she continued, slowly, 'I think it's possible.'

'How can it be possible?' asked Angus, irritably. 'We don't know what we're doing.'

'We don't know what we're doing...*yet*,' Sparks corrected. 'I'll have to figure out the exact details, of course, and draw up a plan of attack; but yes, I think we can do it.'

'You're nuts,' Shug blasted. 'There's no way we can rob three fancy cars from off of a blasted boat and get away with it. It's just not possible.'

'Ship,' said Liam.

'What?' exclaimed Shug, as he was swerved away from what he had been thinking.

'It's a ship,' Liam corrected, 'not a boat. Boats are the ones that go under the water.'

'Since when?' Shug asked, more irritably.

'Since always,' Liam replied.

Shug looked at Sparks, who nodded in agreement. 'Really?' he asked. Sparkes and Liam both nodded in sync. 'Well, I'll be damned. My teachers have a lot to answer for.'

'You're telling us,' Sparks replied, showing all her teeth in amusement.

'If you weren't a girl,' Shug started, 'I'd wrestle you to the ground for that.'

'Who's stopping you?' Sparks answered with a sparkle in her eye. 'Why don't you come over here and do just that?'

This comment made Shug blush bright red, from the top of his face to the souls of his feet.

Sparks, on seeing Shug squirm with embarrassment, decided to leave off of him for a bit. 'Don't you worry,' she said, 'take your time. I can wait.' With that, she gave a cheeky wink at Shug who crumbled.

Liam thought they were going off topic a bit and so decided to bring the conversation back around to the problem at hand. He did not have time to worry about Shug's insecurities or whatever Sparks was trying to pull. He looked to Sparks, 'Do you honestly think you can find a way for us to make this work?' he asked.

Sparks nodded. 'If I can get hold of a few niche items then I even think it likely.'

Liam relaxed slightly 'Well,', he said, 'I was told that if we needed any equipment or anything for the job then we were to ask Ron and he'd sort it out.'

'Fine, then,' Sparks went on, 'I'll make up a list.

Over the next couple of days, Sparks made her plans and her list of specialised items. This was then passed on to Ron by Liam.

Ron was as good as he made out. By the end of the day, everything Sparks had asked for was in their hands, delivered by a small boy, no more than ten years old, on a bright red bicycle. The boy had arrived at the flat at just after seven in the evening, the large package strapped to his back. He said not a single word to Liam when he had answered the door. He simply looked Liam in the face, carefully studying it, before handing over the bulky package. Their business concluded, the boy walked off again. They watched as he climbed back onto his bicycle, from the front window of the flat, and withing the space of thirty seconds, he was gone again.

The four friends had all that they required and, praying that they would not die, got down to specifics. Each of them had their own jobs to do and they spent the remainder of the evening going over them one-by-one, again and again and again, until the plan was burned into their memories.

They went to sleep that night, dreaming of tall ships and fast cars. Even though they now felt that they had a decent plan, they were all still quite nervous. What if it all went wrong? What if they were seen? What if the crew thought it unnecessary to involve the police, reverting to their own ideas of crime and punishment? None of this escaped their tired brains as Hypnos nuzzled them under his tiny wings, opening their young minds up to the field of dreams.

*

The next day, the three friends made themselves as ready as it was possible to be. They went over the plan again, a few times, and prepped themselves for any eventuality they could reasonably envisage. Sparks had made them each up a rucksack, black, and found them some clothes, also black, to aid them in their effort to remain incognito for as long as possible. They all went through their sacks, occasionally pulling out certain things to make inquiries. Sparks carefully explained what everything was, what they were to be used for and how, in fact, they worked.

This all took some time and when they were eventually finished with their prep, it was five in the evening.

'Right, we've got a couple of hours before we head out,' Liam announced. 'I suggest that we order in a chippy or something. Probably best that we eat something before we head out. Who knows when we'll be able to eat again.'

'That's a little pessimistic,' snapped Sparks. 'I've planned this down to a tee. If anything does go wrong then it won't be the theory, it'll be those who are putting it into practice.' She made a point of looking at Angus and Shug.

'Don't look at us,' Shug protested. 'I know what I'm doing.'

'I would hope that we *all* know what we're doing by this point,' sighed Liam. 'Now, what does everyone want to eat from the chippy?'

The gang made their order and filled their bellies once it had arrived, some thirty minutes later. They were as prepared as they would ever be, *almost*. When the others went off to change into their black outfits, Liam knelt down in front of his mother's depiction of Jesus Christ hanging on the cross and closed his eyes. He prayed. He prayed that they would be able to complete their assigned task; he prayed that they would all get out of it intact; and he prayed that there would be no repercussions to come.

As Liam stood up again, he turned to see Sparks watching him from the doorway.

'Don't worry,' she said, calmly. 'I was on my knees as well, earlier.'

This being the most inopportune moment for someone else to turn up, Shug walked through the door behind her. 'What are you two talking about?' he inquired.

'Jealous much?' Sparks asked, blowing him a kiss.

Shug, once again, went bright red and began to stutter. Sparks fed him his blue inhaler and encouraged him to take some long deep breaths.

Just then, Angus came back into the room.

'For goodness' sake,' he said, hotly, 'why don't you two just get a room, already. All this pussyfooting around is getting on my nerves. You like her. She likes you. Get on with it, already, and maybe I can have a best mate that can think in a straight line, again.'

This rant did not just make Shug beam a whole lot brighter but it also caused Sparks, who never usually got embarrassed by anything, turn a slightly darker shade of pink.

'Give it a rest,' Liam scorned, 'and leave them be. I want to go over everything one more time.'

So, they got down to business.

They made sure that they had packed everything they needed; took fifty pounds each, out of the kitty for emergencies; and checked their phones were all at full power. This done, they were finally ready to go. They all breathed deeply, one last time, and walked out the door to face fate and discover their destiny; whatever that might be.

*

Shug had borrowed his cousin's Range Rover Discovery. That evening, the four friends filled the spacious boot with all their sacks and other helpful tools and drove west to the Troon pier. It was a long one. The vast part of the bay was surprisingly shallow and so, in order that the larger ships could dock, a half-mile pier had been built to let them disembark without the use of life-rafts.

The four friends parked up, about five hundred yards away from where the land met the pier and Shug turned off the engine, extinguishing the headlights. They all stared at the carrier ship, lying almost a mile ahead of them.

'Is this going to work?' Liam asked Sparks.

'Certainly, it should,' Sparks answered, softly, 'so long as everyone sticks to the plan.' Again, she looked towards Angus and Shug, one eyebrow raised.

'Okay, then,' Liam continued, trying to avoid any more confrontations, 'let's get this underway.'

'From here on in,' Sparks added, 'it's radio silence from you three, okay?'

The others nodded and they all got out of the car. Walking round to the back, Shug popped the boot and he, Angus and Liam grabbed their respective packs. Black gloves with special waterproof grip sewn into the palms went on; white carnival masks, often seen at masquerade balls, were applied; and boot laces were made secure.

When they were ready, the three of them left Sparks, cross-legged in the boot of the Range Rover, setting up an Alienware laptop. This thirteenth generation i9 powered machine was, in turn, attached to a small generator to give it power, save the battery ran low during the job. A small model helicopter sat next to her. A large juggernaut headlight was attached to the front, stolen of course, and a Bluetooth speaker had been rigged up to the base,

173

between the landing skids. Sparks smiled with satisfaction as she everything to everything else.

Sparks lived for this. Half her life had been dedicated to computers and all that they could do. She was a talented programmer and even built her own machines, stronger and faster than those on the general market. She had decided on a whim, to place the laptop on the list they had sent to Ron, expensive as it was. She had not honestly expected him to agree but get it Ron did and Sparks planned to keep the lot once the job was completed.

When she was done, she pulled out a pair of binoculars and stared through them to the end of the pier. From where she knelt, she could see the three boys slipping off of the pier and into the cold waters. She picked up her phone and dialled a number. Speaking to the person who answered,

Sparks said, 'Operation run-around is a go. I repeat, operation run-around is a go.' She hung up before the recipient could reply.

Adjusting her sites, Sparks observed the men on the ship, along with those patrolling the ramp which ran down to the pier itself. *That must be how they got the cars aboard, in the first place.* Sparks mused.

As she watched, she spotted a couple of youths staggering down towards where the ship was docked. They were singing and waving half empty bottles around in the air as they conducted an invisible orchestra. Two of the men, stationed below the ramp, walked nonchalantly towards them with a mind to direct them away from the ship. This did not go according to plan. After an argument began and one of the guards managed to grab hold of one of the drunks, the other turned and gave out a long, shrill whistle.

That was something that the guards had not been expecting. From around every corner of the dock buildings came a hoard of teenagers, all geared up for a rumble. The mere five guards felt that this was somewhat of a disadvantage and so called out for their colleagues to come down off of the ship to help. This they did. Within a couple of minutes, they were all engulfed by the teenage hoard. Every man fought his hardest but knocking one down, one way, and slapping another who came up in front, while all the time trying to avoid staying in one spot for too long, made the whole experience harrowing to the extreme.

While all this was going on, Liam, Shug and Angus had scaled their way up the anchor chain and climbed aboard. They carefully crept across the deck until they found what they were looking for; three car-sized objects, covered in protective sheets.

Liam, without ceremony, pulled the sheet away from the first one. Underneath was something he had been expecting but still took his breath away. The silver 1973 Porsche AG, 917/30 Spyder was a gem of Germanic perfection and a right wee stunner, to boot. *At a little under four million pounds, it should be*, he thought.

Shug took himself over to the second car and pulled the sheeting off of it, too. Revealed was the one he had been hoping for. The red Lamborghini Veneno Roadster, which came in at around two point eight million pounds, was all that Shug had hoped for. He ran his hand over the bonnet of the Italian beauty, as he cooed over it.

Angus, keen to get his hands on the third attraction, pulled at his sheet. As it flew off in the wind, they all witnessed something extraordinary. The 2020 807-HP, Dodge Charger, Hellcat Redeye SRT would cost a lot less than the other two vehicles. It came in at just over eighty thousand pounds, but the American muscle was no less of a superior quality. With a zero to sixty in three point four seconds, the charger had a top speed of one hundred and ninety-nine miles an hour. Anyone would be counting their blessings to be able to drive that Fiat-Chrysler beast and Angus indeed felt privileged that it should be him behind the wheel over his two companions. The other two could keep their supercars, the Dodge was the car for Angus; it growled just the way that an American muscle car should.

*

Back on dry land, the guards were having a hard time of it. There, however, something that didn't feel quite right about the whole situation. Although the teenage mob had them overwhelmed. Not one of them had done anything to the guards that could be termed as assault. The crowd seemed only to want to have fun at the guards' expense and not actually harm them in any way. When this was realised to them, the guards got a little more confident and started manhandling each and every one of the teenagers whom they could reach.

Just as they were about to do some real damage, a bright light flicked on above them and they herd the overwhelming sound of a helicopter, hovering in the sky. A voice rang out above them. 'This is the Police. Move away from the ramp and place tour hands behind your heads.'

The guard's eyes were blinded by the light as the helicopter moved closer. They did what they were told but the teenagers scattered, each in a different direction.

As the guards cowered on the edge of the dock, the abrupt reverberation of three cars roaring into life overwhelmed the sound of the helicopter and the guards watched in horror as their wards shot off at break-neck speed, down the ramp, around the building and beyond. Withing seconds, they were gone. The helicopter gave the guards one last nudge and they all tumbled into the freezing water, each grabbing on to the others for support. A good job done. The light went out and the noise ended.

The toy helicopter hovered for a second before turning around and heading back towards Sparks and the Range Rover.

*

The boys pulled up at the designated lockups and killed their engines. All three sat still for a moment. They had done it.

Liam still found it hard to believe. It should not have been possible. It would not have been if those other kids hadn't appeared. Liam hoped against hope that Sparks had also managed to get away clean. He would only find out when they got back to Liam's mother's flat. Only then would he be able to relax properly.

Eventually and with a sense of elation, Liam, Shug and Angus left their vehicles where they sat. Wiping down anything they may have touched, they locked up and slipped the keys on top of the rear driver's wheels, as requested. They would be picked up later once the coast was considered clear.

*

Sparks was indeed there, when the three boys returned home. She was sitting in the

181

kitchen, cross-legged on the counter, smoking a spliff. When the boys finally came through the door, she let out a plume of smoke allowing herself to relax.

'We done it, then?' she asked, rhetorically.

Liam let out his own deep breath. 'We did indeed,' he replied.

With that, nothing more was said for at least an hour. They made some tea and toast; smoked a spliff or two; and watched the news, just in case something came up.

'I guess they've not found out, yet,' said Shug, a little disappointed, after they had been watching the same news reels repeating over and over again.

'Either that or the owner doesn't want to get the police involved,' Sparks suggested. 'He may have stolen them, himself. That was quite a lot of security for a shipment nobody was supposed to know about.'

'Maybe,' Liam agreed, 'but they can't bring any of it back onto us. Nobody saw our faces, our fingerprints have been removed from the cars and we left nothing behind. We're free and clear. Well, clear, at least. We still have to free ourselves from Ferguson.'

'I don't see us doing that, any time soon,' Angus tested.

'Again, maybe,' said Liam. 'We just have to find a way out before it's too late.'

They all agreed with that. None of them liked Ferguson and they hated being under his thumb. It may even get to the point where they would have no choice than to take their chances and run.

Shug's pocket began to vibrate. He pulled his phone from out of his pocket pressed a couple of buttons and dropped it on the coffee table. 'Hey cousin of mine,' he said, 'I have you on speaker.'

A clear voice spoke from inside the phone, 'Hi there, Shuggy, me old mate. How'd it go?'

Shug didn't need to ask what he meant. 'Spectacularly,' he replied. 'We all got away clean and the items in question are on their way to wherever it is they're destined for.'

'Excellent,' the voice congratulated, 'hope we were able to help enough.'

'Yeah, mate, that was proper of you. If you and your mates hadn't distracted the guards and got them all off of the ship at the same time, I don't know what we would have done. You're golden.'

'Marvelous,' the voice continued. Glad it all went well. I'll pick up the Range Rover in the morning.'

'How about you make it late afternoon,' Shug suggested. 'I'm knackered and don't plan to be out of bed before three.'

'Fair enough,' conceded the voice. 'I rather think you deserve it. I'll let you go now, though; got to see a man about a dog. See you the morrow.'

'See ya,' Shug confirmed. He hung up the phone and placed it back into his pocket.

The others were all staring at him with big grins on their faces.

'What is it?' Shug asked.

'*Shuggy?*' Sparks queried.

This gave Shug more embarrassment than he needed in one night. 'It's a family pet name, okay?' he blabbed. 'Nobody outside of the immediate family get to use it, all right?'

'Fair enough,' Liam agreed, still smiling, '*Shuggy.*'

Shug near went for him. Liam held his hand up in mock defence. 'Last time, I promise,' he said, almost in hysterics. 'Now, how's about we get our chong on and play some GTA.'

This sounded like a plan. They set up the console and sat there for the rest of the night, setting aside their troubles for a short time.

As Time Goes By

The next few days were quiet. The four friends kept pretty much to themselves, with the only people they spoke to were the Sri Lankan gentleman who ran the corner shop and the pizza-faced delivery boy who brought them their food, each night. They were all exhausted, both mentally and physically, by the event which I have just relayed and a few days of well-deserved rest and relaxation was just what they all needed. They had decided, on the day following the raid, to keep themselves inside Liam's mother's flat for the foreseeable future. They only left their comfort zone when they absolutely had to. Spending their time playing games and watching movies, they managed to bring their flagging spirits back to something resembling normalcy.

Liam made a point of going out on only two other occasions, as he could not allow himself to leave his mother alone in the hospital for any length of time. He was not able to hold up much more of a conversation than she was, so he sat there and read to her from her old and battered copy of the Bible; the Roman Catholic approved CTS. She spoke little while Liam was with her, but to request that he read through the book of Proverbs. He found some of it a bit hard going but he did notice several things repeated. One thing that kept coming up was how to behave to one's parents. He loved his mother and had always respected her and would do anything he could to spare her all pain. His father, however, could rot in Hell, for all Liam cared but, according to Proverbs, that was not the right way to think. Apparently, you not only had to keep your body from sin but also your mind and therefore, your soul.

One of the verses that he noticed was, '...*a child left to himself brings shame to his mother.*' He was finding that, on this point at least, the good book had got it right. It hadn't been long after his mother had entered the hospital before Liam found himself in debt to Ferguson. Admittedly, Liam had stolen the car before then but that was just semantics; he had only started actually working for Ferguson proper, after the fact.

Another verse that Liam noticed was, '*Listen to your father, who gave you life, and do not despise your mother when she is old.*' Liam could not even imagine despising his mother. She was a wonderful woman and nobody could help getting old or sick. He loved her and always would, even after she was gone. On the other side of the coin, he could not think of anything his father could say that Liam would be interested in listening to. The man had left them alone and bereft. What could he possibly have to say that would make that all okay? *Sod all*, Liam thought.

One other verse, which his mother reacted to more than the whole of the rest of the book, was a line that said, '*If one curses his father or his mother, his lamp will be put out in utter darkness.*' Why would his mother react to this particular verse? Liam certainly felt like his life was currently in darkness but his father had deserted her, just as much as the swine had abandoned Liam. *She should hate the bastard*, Liam thought, and not wish Liam to refrain from cursing him. When she had heard it, Liam's mother slid her hand over slightly, so that it was resting upon Liam's. She had smiled at him. She had nodded. Why? This was not the actions of someone who had been deprived of a husband for all these years.

Whatever her motives, Liam's mother appeared to be trying to push him towards his father. She was not long for this world, as previously noted, but surely she did not wish for him to go and live with his father, in her absence. He barely knew the man. Liam did not know what exactly he did for a living. He owned the Ginger Nightcap, of course, but supposedly, he had some other kind of work. What this was, Liam had no clue.

Liam could only hope that it did not come to that. He was managing to save up some money from the deals and the theft from the ship. Whether he would be able to earn enough from that, to pay his rent and eat properly, was still to be seen. Once he was out from under Ferguson's feet, he would have to get a job. Liam shivered at the thought of it.

If it came down to it and he had no other option but to make good with his father, Liam knew he would have to bite the bullet but he prayed that he would never have to make that decision.

Open All Hours

It had been four months since they had first started working for Ferguson. So far, they had managed to navigate their way through the dangers and stresses of the criminal life. The weed business had grown rapidly and now they were selling a kilo of the finest skunk every week. They had also been surprised but relieved that their first real grand theft auto job had gone successfully. Ferguson had received the three cars and, by what Ron had told them, had been delighted with their performance. Liam was simply waiting, now. He knew, in the depths of himself, that the thievery would not be a one-time event. Every day, he would check his phone to see if there were any new messages.

When Ron did contact them again, he did not call. It was three in the morning and

Liam had just fallen asleep after a night up drinking with the other three. He was woken by someone banging on the door. Answering it, with the chain still attached for safety sake, he saw Ron and Charlie, standing there like well-dressed gorillas.

'Do you know what time it is?' Liam asked, rubbing his eyes and yawning.

'For Mr Ferguson,' Ron had answered, 'yer open a' hours. Now, open the door.'

It was then that Liam noticed Ferguson standing behind them. *Damn*, he thought, *this can't be good*.

It was not. Liam invited them in, not wishing to have hardened gangsters hanging out outside his flat for too long. Whence inside, they all sat down in the sittingroom, Charlie dragging Shug off of the couch and manhandling Angus away from his spot by the fire. It was then that Sparks walked through, rubbing her eyes, wearing nothing but a black t-shirt that would have required another three inches to reach her knees. 'What's all the noise about?' she began to say, before she saw who was sitting in Liam's mother's chair. 'Oh,' she finished.

'Ah,' Ferguson grinned. 'I see we are all here. That is providential. It'll save time in the explaining of things.'

The boys were directed to stand by the fire, in their boxers and Sparks was told to sit down on the couch beside Liam. She tried her best to hike down the t-shirt as much as she could but quickly realised that a crossing of the legs was in order. Liam looked at her face which was a picture of disgust and felt her pain. This was not something the sixteen-year-old should have to deal with. It was bad enough that Ferguson had them all under his thumb but to put Sparks, the only girl in the room, through such embarrassment was not playing the game. If Liam was not so scared, he would have said something colourful to Ferguson. As it stood, all he could bring himself to say was, 'Do you mind if Sparks puts some clothes on?'

Ferguson thought about this, his eyes where they should not be. After a few seconds, he nodded and Sparks ran out of the room to get dressed. It was a few minutes before she returned and that time was spent in silence, as Charlie and Ron made themselves at home in the kitchen.

When they eventually came out, again, Charlie was carrying a tray. 'There you go, Mr Ferguson, sir,' Charlie said as he passed a cup of tea and a slice of malt loaf to his employer. Then joining Ron at the doorway, the pair of them stood tall with their hands clasped, smartly in front of them.

Once everyone was where Ferguson wanted them to be, he begun to talk. 'Okay, I think we are ready to begin.'

The others looked on expectedly.

'I was profoundly impressed with your performance at the Troon docks,' he continued. 'I have received the items in question and was pleased to see that there was not so much as a scratch on any of them. Very well done.'

The four friends started to relax a little. If this was why he was here then it was all for the good. *Mind you*, Liam thought, looking at the clock on the mantlepiece, *it's quarter-past-three in the morning.*

Ferguson spoke some more. 'I now feel that you have, most assuredly, proven yourselves and have shown that you can work well in a stressful situation. I therefore have another small job for you. There *will* be more to come.'

Liam managed to find his voice, again. 'Another car theft?' he asked, as politely as he could.

'No, my dear boy,' Ferguson corrected. 'You are to find your way to Glasgow Green and enter the People's Palace, surreptitiously. There is a small item that I wish to have in my possession. Just a trinket but something that I crave.'

'What is it? Sparks asked, now fully dressed and less self-conscious.

Ferguson smiled at her. 'In one of the museum's sections, there is a room with an orange floor and walls painted green and yellow. In this room there is a chair. On that chair, you will find a map. This is what I want you to retrieve.'

'A map?' queried Liam.

'Indeed,' Ferguson replied. 'The current management believe that it is merely a prop but I have it on good authority that it is, in fact, an original which was found in eighteen hundred and ninety-eight. It was discovered in one of the attic rooms and the original caretaker thought it would be nice to include it in the museum. It is supposed to have been extremely old even then. Now, I cannot think how much it could be worth.'

The four friends sat in silence, not wanting to believe what they were going to be expected to do.

'This is not the reason I wish it, of course,' Ferguson went on. 'I have no intention of ever selling the piece. This will go into my own personal collection and there it shall stay until the point of my death. It is not just a piece of history but the artist who drew it is, in my humble opinion, a genius in cartography.'

'How come you know so much about this piece, if it's been sitting on that chair, untouched for so long?' Liam asked, with due care.

Ferguson's teeth gleamed in pleasure. 'You have a good mind, son. I shall tell you. There is a gentleman whose grandfather was one of the first to begin working in the museum, back when it was first instituted. He told his son of the map, for purely entertainment's sake. His son, in turn, told his own son. This man is the one who told me... *eventually.*'

Liam, remembering the room under Ferguson's restaurant, winced at the thought of the poor grandson being tortured at the hands of Ron and Charlie.

'So, you want us to steal this map?' Sparks inquired, seeking confirmation of something she did not wish to believe.

Ferguson smiled for a third time. 'Indeed, my dear. That is exactly what I wish and exactly what I expect you to do. You have

200

shown what you are capable of when you put your minds to it and I fully expect that you will be successful. If not… well, we shall cross that bloody stream when we come to it.' His smile had gone away.

The four friends all looked at each other, willing the other three to come up with some reasonable explanation for why they could not possibly do what Ferguson was asking of them.

Liam thought of one. 'What about the security?'

'Oh,' Ferguson replied, 'I don't think there is anything there that young Georgia can't bypass.'

The use of Spark's real name made her cringe. Nobody, not even her parents used that name in reference to her, anymore; except for her maternal grandmother, of course. She would never take to calling Sparks by her chosen name. To her, she would always be *wee Georgie*. Apart from that, she had banished it from her life, years previously and was therefore somewhat surprised that Ferguson knew what it was.

This aside, they all tried their best to come up with some way to get out of robbing one of the oldest museums in Glasgow. It was to no avail. They could not think of anything that would cause Ferguson to change his mind. They would just have to resign themselves to the fact that the job was going to happen. Nothing they could do or say would change this.

Their conversation completed to Ferguson's satisfaction, the three gentlemen left the flat as smoothly as when they had entered. Liam, Sparks, Shug and Angus, all sat in their respective seats for some time, after that. They were all shocked, tired and still a little drunk from their previous session. It was not until Angus got up and knelt down at the coffee table and started to roll a spliff that the other three begun to slip out of their trance.

'Damn,' was all Liam could say. There was nothing else that *could* be said. Therefore, they all sat there, in silence. They each considered their individual options, as they passed the spliff between them, from right to left and back to Angus who finished it. Shug then took it upon himself to roll a second and the cycle repeated, once again, and again, and again, until they were all caked and dreaming of better times when they weren't expected to rob cargo ships or art museums.

Spaced

For four days, the four friends looked over the maps, building plans, notes and photographs. At first, they didn't have a clue what they were going to do. The job seemed impossible. Even if it weren't impossible, it would surely take someone with better skills than them to pull it off. The biggest thing they had ever done was to steal the three cars from the ship. In the end it had not been that difficult. This job, however, was something else, entirely. This was not going to be easy. The museum's cutting-edge security system was set up so that this should be so.

It was not until the evening on the second day that Sparks thought she had found a way to bypass the security measures; the electronic ones, at least.

Liam had been surprised at this. 'I thought you said that it was all on a closed loop, or something?' he asked.

'It is,' Sparks agreed, 'but if I can get onto the grounds and work my way round to this point,' she indicated a position on the map, 'then I can plug directly in. No need for wireless.'

Shug furled his eyebrows. 'What about the guards? I hope you haven't forgotten about them. I think it said on the sheet that they patrol in such a way as no point is unobserved for more than five minutes.'

'You're right,' she granted, 'but I think I can do enough in that time to switch everything off and keep it that way. I'll even pop a new passcode onto it. That way they'll not be able to regain control of anything.'

'You still have to give yourself time to get away again, though,' Liam reminded her.

'I think I can do it,' Sparks begged, 'please, let me try.'

Liam gave Shug a queried look. He didn't look sure. There was no point asking Angus. He looked like didn't know what was going on. Liam was becoming worried. Angus had been smoking more and more, recently. He really had to lay off it for a while or there was no telling how it could affect their nefarious affairs. His face shone with an air of happy resignation. This was not good when planning a robbery.

Liam turned his attentions back to Sparks. 'Fine, then, you can give it a shot. However, when I call time on it, you stop and run, *instantly*; whatever you might be in the middle of, agreed?'

'Fine, I promise,' Sparks consented.

Liam sighed. 'Okay, then. We go in at night. Shug, give your cousin a call and ask if we can get a loan of his car again. You can drop the rest of us off at this fountain, on the corner of Arcadia and Green.' He pointed to a spot on the map not far away from the entrance to the museum grounds. 'You can then park up at the McPhun's carpark. As soon as you get there, switch off your engine, duck down and wait. Whatever else you do, don't leave the car. You'll need to be ready to pick us up again when we come out. We may have people after us by that point and we won't be able to hang around waiting.'

Shug agreed to the terms and they went on to discuss the actual break-in. They found the route that Liam and Angus would take on the building plans, if Sparks was indeed able to grant them the entry they required. If they could gain access to the camera feeds as well then that would allow them to avoid any and all guards who might happen their way. If they could manage all that, they would indeed begin to imagine that they could truly complete the job with a modicum of success.

That all decided, they made the list of things which they would require and Liam made his way down to the Keys to pass it on to Ron who would arrange for them to be delivered back to Liam's mum's flat.

Afterwards, they relaxed and played some video games. They also had a little smoke to calm their nerves. Angus had more than most.

In the end. Liam took himself to bed; Shug and Sparks made their way, silently to the spare room; and Angus was left where he was, curled up in front of the fire with one fist, balled up under his head as a makeshift pillow.

The next day was Liam's birthday. Not having any time to celebrate, the other three told him that they would throw a big bash after the job was done. Liam was not too bothered, if he were being honest. His mother was not even able to open her eyes or speak, anymore. It would not be long before he had to start making a difficult decision. The fact that his father was no father at all, did not help. What was there to celebrate but for his three loyal friends? He would be spending time with them whatever they did, which was all that mattered. It would just have been better if they had not been planning a robbery.

That evening, Ron arrived, in person, with all that they had requested. They had not expected this. The last time, a young boy had been the carrier. Liam and the others thought this must be to keep the two parties apart as much as possible. Yet, there he was, in plain sight, carrying two large bags, one in each hand.

'I just wanted to mak sure ye a' huv this unner control,' he twanged. 'It's a gey big joab, this. I need yous tae tell me fit, if ony'hing, you think will gang wrang.'

'What could possibly gang warang,' Angus mocked, still a little stoned from his latest spliff.

Ron rounded on the young lad in a second. 'Dinnae ye tak the piss oot o' me, pal. I'll huv yer fuckin' heid on a platter. Got it?'

'I think so,' Angus grinned, pulling out his mobile phone. 'Let me just get my translator up and I'll let you know.'

Ron turned on Liam. 'Get that wee prick in order, or I will. Understand?'

Liam had a lot more self-control than Angus. 'I'll sort it,' Liam replied.

'Ye'd better,' Ron warned as he got up and went to the door. 'I dinnae want tae be the wan tae resign ye all, permanently.'

That was a funny term to use, Liam had all thought, after Ron left the flat in his wake, but it was more than clear what he meant.

When they were alone, Sparks turned on Angus with purest rage. 'That is most definitely it,' she cried. 'You don't get any more smoke or drink until this job is over. I'm not having you bollocks this all up for us.'

Angus drew a look of pure shock and great concern on his face. 'But that's ages away,' he cried.

'It's only another twenty-four hours,' Liam sighed. 'One day! I'm sure you can manage to go one bloody day without having a spliff.'

'That would be fine if I was allowed a beer or two but I can't even do that.' Angus started to cry for real, 'why are you all doing this to me?'

'We're not doing it *to* you,' Shug joined in, 'we're doing it *for* you. Understand? It's for your own benefit, just as much as it is for all of ours.'

Angus rubbed his eyes. 'I don't need to hang around with people who won't even let me have a fly puff. That's not what I call friendship.' He stood up, unsteadily and grabbed his jacket. 'Sod yous all,' he stated. 'I don't need any of you.' He then staggered out of the flat and he was gone. None of the other three went any further than the doorway, in their attempts to call him back.

'Forget him,' Sparks moaned, as she put on the kettle. 'He can do what he likes.'

Liam was concerned, though. 'But it does mean that we're now one man short for the robbery.'

'He would only have mucked things up, in any case. We'll be better off without him.'

Shug didn't like the way the conversation was going. 'He's still our mate,' he said, slipping on his own coat, 'well, mine at least.' With that, he stalked Angus out into the cold.

'Should we not go after him?' Liam asked of Sparks.

He only got a derisive snort in reply. 'If he wants to go out chasing that wee tit, he has every right to do so. Far be it for me to stop him.'

Liam was unsure about what they should do about the job which now seemed to be destined to fail before they had even begun. They were, at the very least, one man down; possibly two. If Shug did not come back, they would have no chance of making it work. If that became the case, they would have to inform Ferguson that they were unable to do what he asked. *Before swiftly leaving the country*, he added in the quiet of his own head. The south of France had always appealed to him. Liam considered that it may be a little more difficult to cross borders now that Brexit had finally taken effect but they would have no other option but to try. Maybe jump on one of those migrant boats as they head back across the channel.

With all that had just occurred, Liam thought it prudent to go to his bed and have an early night. If they were still able to do the job, he would need his beauty sleep. He left Sparks where she stood, resolutely staring out of the window, for any hint of Shug's return.

*

The next day, Liam awoke to find that Shug had given up looking for Angus and returned to the flat. He and Sparks were curled up on the couch when Liam walked into the sittingroom. 'Tea, anyone?' he asked, calmly, as if nothing had happened.

The other two shook their heads. Liam took this to mean that they did not want to talk, so he made himself a cuppa and sat at the kitchen table, as he attempted the crossword in the previous week's Daily Record.

When four o'clock came around, Liam looked up at the face of Sparks. She had walked into the kitchen, flicked on the kettle and looked back at Liam. 'We're doing it,' she said.

Liam could not think what to say. He decided on, 'Fair enough,' and left it at that.

Sparks sat down next to Liam at the table and breathed, slowly and deeply. 'We'll keep most of the plan as it was,' she went on. 'The only differences will be that Shug will go in with you, instead of Angus, and we'll just

215

have to keep the car closer by, so that we can have a quick getaway. Shug suggested that we leave the keys on top of the driver's wheel. That way whoever is back first can get it started and be ready to go. It'll probably be me, in any case. Even without that wee... *I won't say the word*, we still have a good chance of getting this right. Maybe more so.'

'I still don't like it,' Liam sighed, 'but I don't suppose we have any other option. It's not like we can just say to Ferguson, *we're not doing it*, is it? He'll have us all in concrete wellies, before the night is out.'

'Exactly,' Sparks agreed. 'We have no choice. It must be done and this is now the only way we can do it. We just have to get our heads down and stick to the plan.'

'Remember, that includes you,' Liam reminded the tempestuous girl. 'If I say run, you run, okay?'

Sparks agreed and they began to get themselves ready. Half an hour later, Shug left the flat so he could retrieve his cousin's car. When he returned with it, he told the others what the cousin had said. 'If we muck this up, Shug explained, 'he's going to report the car stolen, so we won't have much time to escape, if that happens.'

'What a wee...' Sparks begun.

'Don't,' Shug warned. 'He's only looking out for his own business. He can't have the police thinking his car was used in a robbery without a good explanation. If he gets caught helping us, he's in for more time than the three of us put together. He's got previous.'

No more needed to be said. The simple word, *previous*, was one that commanded special dispensation. Nobody wanted to be the cause of Shug's cousin going to the jail.

That would not rest well on their consciences.

'And if he goes inside, then how long do you think it'll be before someone else takes over his patch. Not long, I can tell you. It's a minefield out there. You have to cling on tight if you want to keep your standing in society. He'll have next to nothing when he comes out. He won't even have his car 'cos the polis will take it from him.'

'Fine, then,' Sparks conceded. 'Let's just make sure we don't have anything go wrong.'

The other two consented, wholeheartedly and they set off in the borrowed Range Rover.

*

When they arrived at the spot, next to the fountain, they got a real and very much unwanted surprise. It was Liam who spotted it first. 'Look over there,' he announced. 'There's someone lying out on the grass, under the fountain.'

'Don't tell me,' Spark groaned, 'it's that wee bandit, isn't it?'

'I thought you didn't want me to tell you,' asked Liam.

"Stop being so bloody obtuse,' blasted Sparks. 'Is it him or isn't it?'

Liam looked back at the dozing figure, as a plumb of smoke arose from a hooded head. 'I very much think it is.' Liam groaned.

Even Shug was not happy with this new information. 'Damn it,' he yelled, 'what the hell's he doing, here?'

The three friends pulled up at the side of the road and called, softly to Angus. On hearing that he was no longer alone, Angus sat up, looked at the people who had known his name and smiled. 'You made it,' he exclaimed. 'Excellent.'

'No,' whispered Sparks, as they got out of the car and sidled up to the young stoner, 'not excellent. What *do* you think you are doing?'

'You didn't think I would leave you to do this job alone, did you. I've got my share in this, just as much as all of yous.'

'Well, you're not going inside, I can tell you that, right now.' The fact that these words came out of the mouth of Shug hurt Angus more than anything before.

'What do I do, then?' he whimpered.

'You can stay in the car and bring it around when we call,' Shug ordered. 'I'm not having you muck this up.'

'And no more spliffs until we're out of here,' Liam added. 'That's non-negotiable.'

Angus mournfully acceded and pinged the remaining end of his spliff into the fountain's moat.

'There' Angus proclaimed, 'all gone.'

'And no lighting another,' said Sparks, casting in her own two cents. 'Doesn't matter how long we're in there, you stick to the fags, okay?'

Angus held up his hands in protestation. 'Okay, okay,' he said. 'I get the idea.'

Once Angus had driven off in the car, towards the carpark, Liam faced Sparks and asked the all-important question. 'Are you sure you can do this in under five minutes?'

Sparks proclaimed that she could and they all moved, soft-footedly up the Green Road, past the help centre on their left. Twenty yards later, they hopped off the road, to their right and padded across the grass, trying their best to keep to the shadows. With the night being dark and all

221

the streetlights in this particular area being extinguished by nine in the evening, they had little trouble keeping themselves unseen as they made their way to the back of the building.

When they reached the Colton Weavers' Gate, they slipped through and they were at the point where Sparks needed to be.

In an attempt to gain Sparks as much time as possible, the three friends had established themselves inside a bush, close by. When one of the guards came around the corner, they all held their breath. He wandered around for a minute, nodded to himself at a satisfactory sweep, ignited the end of a cigarette and turned back the way he had come.

No sooner was his back turned, than Sparks was out of the bush and sprinting across to the hook-up point. She had it open and was pulling out wires of many colours before the man even turned the corner.

'She *is* fast,' Liam announced.

'She is that' Shug agreed, smiling. 'Nobody better.'

'Let's hope not.'

The two boys, however, couldn't wait around to find out. As soon as the guard had turned the corner, they ran off to their chosen point of entry. When Sparks gave them the proverbial nod, they smashed the glass door and dashed inside, hiding behind the doors that led to the corridor. When the guards came in to see what all the noise was about, Liam and Shug slipped out behind them and made their escape through the palace, itself.

They managed to find the room quickly enough and the map was indeed laying on the chair, to the left of the fire. Liam grabbed it, rolled it up and shoved it into a storage tube and deposited it in his backpack.

'Quick,' Shug whispered, 'we need to get out of here, smartish.'

They left the room with haste and were heading back down the corridor when Shug's phone started to vibrate.

'I'm so glad you remembered to put that on silent,' Liam remarked.

'It's Sparks,' he replied, simply. Answering the phone, he listened carefully. 'Damn it,' he cursed. 'I'll kill the wee shite.'

As it transpired, Angus had not been able to keep to his promise and had been spotted by two patrol officers, as he lay on the bonnet of the Range Rover, puffing away, wishing to keep the inside of the car free from the smell. He had been thrown into the back of the police car and more officers were on their way. Sparks had seen one of the policemen talking to a passing guard. He must have informed the officer that their security was down. This was something the police would take very seriously and the three friends knew that they had to find a way out as quickly as possible.

'Sparks,' Shug spoke seriously, 'you get out of there, now!'

'But what about you two?' she asked, worried.

'Never mind us,' Shug soothed. 'We'll be fine, just get going. *NOW.*'

He hung up the phone and stared at Liam. 'We're screwed, aren't we?' he said taking a pull of his inhaler.

Liam nodded. 'I think that may well be the case.'

A noise came from down the corridor that made them jump and they observed three mean-looking guards running around the corner, towards them.

'Quick,' Liam shouted, 'this way.'

225

Liam dragged Shug away from the oncoming storm and up a set of spiral stairs that lead to the roof. When they were up there, they blocked off the door with a steel pole before darting around the roof's perimeter, searching for a safe way down.

'I think we can manage down the drainpipe,' Shug suggested. 'I certainly can't see any other way we're going to get down.

Liam looked at the proposed route and back to the blocked-off door which was quickly becoming unstable. The guards would break through soon and Liam, for one, did not wish to still be standing there when they did.

'Fine, then' he settled, 'go on then.'

Shug went first and once he was a third of the way down, Liam followed. Everything was going well, until Liam's hand slipped from its grasp and he fell to the ground, knocking Shug as he plunged downwards.

The two of them were lying on the ground when they heard Sparks shouting out to them. She had retrieved the Range Rover, which the police had mistakenly left unattended, and was now driving at speed, straight towards them.

It was not enough. As the Range Rover came within ten yards of the boys, three police cars, sirens blaring, blocked off any hope of escape. They were all caught. It was the end.

We're dead, Liam thought to himself, as the paramedics placed the handcuffed boy on the portable gurney and slid him into the back of an ambulance.

As Liam lay in the hospital bed, that night, chained to the side bars, he wondered where it had all gone wrong and how they were ever getting out of the mess Angus had gotten them into.

As he slept, Liam dreamed of fishing boats and concrete wellies.

Yes, Minister

It had been a difficult night. The next morning, the four friends had been taken down to the local police station where Sparks was separated from the others. Liam, Shug and Angus were dragged through the corridors to an interview room and left there. It was not until two hours had passed that the door reopened, allowing a detective in a plain navy-blue suit to enter. There was a table in the middle of the room. Three chairs ran down one side of it. The detective indicated for them to seat themselves on them, as he rested himself on another, positioned opposite.

'Well, well, well,' the detective exclaimed, slowly, flicking through a file.

'I didn't know you guys actually said things like that,' grinned Angus.

Shug, who was seated next to the young fool, jabbed his elbow into Angus' ribs, whispering, 'Shut it, smartarse,' out of the corner of his mouth.

Angus went instantly quiet.

'I see that at least one of you has a modicum of sense in their head,' the detective deduced. 'Perhaps you can learn from him. Now,' he resumed as he continued to flick through the file, 'you are all going to be charged on a number of counts. Let me see, yes, there's trespassing; illegal access to electronic data; breaking and entering; destruction of property; human endangerment; attempted suicide; and resisting arrest. Oh, and one count of marijuana possession.' He looked up at this point. 'Have I got that about right? Have I missed anything out?' the detective laid the file down on the table, next to the offending map which he had also brought along.

'No comment,' Liam replied, before Angus could open his mouth and get them into even more trouble.

'I see,' sighed the detective. You do realise that you're in a lot of trouble? Now, I'm sure that it wasn't one of you three that came up with the idea of robbing the Palace. You're not the type. Why don't you just tell me who it was that asked you to steal this map? It'll go better for you. If you were coerced into doing it then you may be able to get a reduced sentence. I'll even put a good word in for you, myself. How about that?'

The three boys stared at him, blankly. Their faces showing no emotion; except for Angus who was trying not to cry. Shug had a tight grip on his friend's kneecap. He was of the belief that Angus needed a little applied pressure, sometimes, if he were going to act right. This was one of those occasions and Shug was not going to let go until the interview was over.

The detective came to the realisation that he was not going to get anything out of the three boys. He gathered up the file and the map and stood up. 'Well,' he said, 'a Constable will be in shortly to take your fingerprints and a DNA swab. You'll then be taken to the cells, for the night. In the morning we shall see about finding you a public defender.'

All being said that was going to be said, the detective left the room and locked it behind him.

*

Five hours later, all three of them had walked out of the station with no charges but for the one count of marijuana possession.

That had surprised them. Before their release, they had been taken to the interview room, once again. There, they waited, expecting some inexperienced public defender to come in and tell them how much shit they were really in. What actually happened was strange. Instead of the public defender, they were greeted by a tall, slim woman in a very expensive-looking, pin-striped, dress-suit. She had spoken a few, hushed words to the detective and marched them out of the station. This, she did in a matter of three minutes. What she said to the detective that allowed them the freedom of breathing in fresh air, was beyond their understanding. They were, however, very grateful.

'She was bloody brilliant,' Angus expressed, as the woman left them on the street, without so much as a word about why she had helped them.

'She was certainly something,' Shug agreed. 'Who do you think she was?'

'I have an idea,' Liam groaned, 'but you're not going to like it.'

*

Indeed, they did not like it and, as Liam had expected, they were all cogently summoned to meet with Ferguson, the next day, this time in his own home.

They were all collected from their respective homes. Four black BMW's had been sent out, in order that Ferguson could be sure that each and every one of them would attend. When Liam got into the vehicle designated for him, the partition that separated the driver from the rear passengers was closed so that the driver was hidden from view. The windows were also blacked-out on the inside as well as the

234

outside. Nobody could see in and Liam could not see out. It was like a tiny jailcell.

Due to not having any way of knowing where they were going, Liam spent the journey with his eyes closed. If he were to be forced to spend that time in solitude, then he was going to have a nap. Liam was still sore from falling off the museum roof and the last few weeks, months even, had been intense and arduous. Liam had, therefore, taken to getting in a few hours shut eye whenever he was able. At that point he *was* able; so sleep, he did.

He was only roused again when the car came to a complete stop and the right passenger door was opened. Revealed in the blinding daylight, was the same woman who had orchestrated their release.

'Mr Ferguson will see you, now,' was all she said to him, before she walked off towards the main doors of an enormous mansion.

It was clear to Liam that she expected him to follow, so he slipped out of the BMW and limped after her.

On entering the mansion, Liam was astounded at all the art and sculptures which were scattered around. It seemed to Liam that Ferguson must have spent most of his adult life searching for and acquiring all those pieces. They must have been worth a great deal more than the proverbial pretty penny.

The woman steered Liam through the vestibule and down a corridor, to the left. At the end of said corridor, they entered a large sittingroom which contained two black leather sofas; a glass coffee table, which sat between them; and many glass cases which contained a great many more antiques and artefacts. Liam could not tell what any of them were or why Ferguson deemed them to be important to him but he had made damned sure that they were all kept dust-free and securely locked. On the floor, under the table, was an oriental style rug. Liam doubted that it had been bought at the local B&Q outlet. Spill something on that and you could not simply drive it down to the local dry cleaners. Real professionals would have to be called in; expensive ones.

On the opposite wall from the door they entered by, there were a large set of patio doors, leading to a perfectly cultivated lawn. From what Liam could see, it was large enough to be able to fit an Olympic size swimming pool. All Ferguson had desired to place there was a small fountain, right in the centre.

Liam had been the last to arrive. On one of the large sofas, sat Sparks, Shug and Angus. None of them were in a very good mood. Liam could see the strain in their faces as they attempted to hide this from their host.

Ferguson, himself, was standing at the fireplace, one foot on the hearth as he rested an arm on the mantlepiece. He was sipping on a glass of whisky that, Liam assumed, probably cost more than his mother's flat.

'Ah, Mr Macrae, please join us,' greeted Ferguson, jovially directing him to the near-filled sofa.

Liam obediently sat down, glancing at the others who were a picture of distress. Angus' knee was jumping up and down at a rapid rate.

Ferguson walked over to the opposing couch and laid his glass on the table. Another man, whom Liam had not noticed before then, stepped out from behind a set of bookcases. He was not the type of man whom Liam, or any of the others, would have imagined witnessing in the den of a major drug dealer and long-time thief. He was of average height; wore a black suit and a shirt to match; and adorned that shirt with what has come to be known as a dog collar. *A bloody priest*, Liam thought. What's he doing here? He hoped against hope that it wasn't for last rights.

Ferguson must have realised what Liam was thinking because he then introduced the visitor.

'My friends,' he said, 'please let me introduce you to the Reverend Thomas O'Neal.'

Ah, Liam thought, *a Protestant, then.*

The minister nodded his recognition to the for youths. 'I shall leave you to business,' he said to Ferguson. As he made to leave, he glanced back at the four friends. 'Now, you all be good for William,' he said, smiling.

239

'Yes, minister,' Liam replied.

'It's Reverend,' the minister corrected, 'not minister. Minister is the job description and Reverend is the title.' He paused. 'I'm assuming that you were brought up a Catholic?'

'Yes, Reverend,' Liam replied, ever a quick learner. 'Our Lady of Mount Carmel.'

'Ah,' the minister acknowledged, 'yes. Good church. Father Martin is the permanent there, I believe. Very nice man. Very good priest.'

'Yes, Reverend,' Liam repeated. '*He* is a good man.'

'And when was the last time you attended Mass, child?' the minister inquired, un-noticing of Liam's inflection.

'It's been eight years since my last confession,' Liam rolled off, automatically. 'Not since my father walked out on us.'

The minister sighed. 'I see. I would suggest that you do not spurn the Lord our God because of that which man has done. Please think about returning. I'm sure Father Martin would be pleased to see you again.'

Liam was confused. 'But you're a Protestant, aren't you? Should you not be trying to convert me or something?'

'We are all one in the Lord,' the minister replied. 'To be honest, there is not much of a difference between Roman Catholicism and true Catholicism; the latter being us,' he smiled a cheeky smile. 'It's primarily down to how we view communion and the extra mysticism which your lot add on to what the gospels teach us. So long as you are being taught from the good book, as truthfully as the priest is able, then God will not mind if ye be Catholic or Protestant.'

'What does he think about liberating museum pieces?' Angus asked, completely in character.

Ferguson glared at the boy but the minister merely smiled. 'I think that would be an ecumenical decision,' he stated.

The ultimate get-out clause, Liam thought.

Before Angus or any of the others were able to debate this comment, Reverend O'Neal nodded to Ferguson and left the room, followed by one of the in-house security men. After that, the only people left in the room were the four friends, Ferguson and the woman.

'Okay, then,' Ferguson spoke, after the door had closed again, 'I think it is time that we get down to business.' He sat down opposite them and retrieved his glass, again.

The four friends stared at him in anticipation. The woman, calm as anything, walked over to the wet bar and made herself a drink.

'I have been informed,' Ferguson accused, 'that you four made a complete hash of what was asked of you. This is mostly, I might add, down to the incompetence of young Mr Macdonald, here.' He pointed his glass at Angus, who grimaced.

Liam tried his best to soften the issue. 'I'm sorry, Mr Ferguson, sir,' he said. 'I don't know what to tell you.'

'You don't need to tell me anything,' Ferguson replied, sternly. 'I know exactly what occurred and why. Mr Macdonald got so stoned that he allowed himself to be apprehended by the police. This meant that the police were on site to get the news of the break-in relayed to them by a wandering guard. Police and guards then chased you two through the museum,' at this point he indicated that he was talking to Liam and

Shug. 'After which, you both jumped off the roof, like the idiots that you are and collapsed on the ground as if you had just been shot. Miss Smith, here, also made the mistake of returning for you both. She should have scarpered at the first sign of trouble. Never go back. Cardinal rule, as they say.'

We *are* really sorry,' Liam tried again.

'I'm sure you are,' Ferguson accepted, 'but that is not good enough. I shall be expecting you all to make this up to me, and soon.'

The four friends all groaned in time with each other.

'What was that you said?' asked Ferguson. 'Come on, speak up.'

'Of course, Mr Ferguson,' they chorused, 'we promise.'

'Good,' Ferguson acknowledged, 'now, Ron will be at your flat at seven PM, tomorrow night with details on how you can fulfil this promise.'

The group all gave a synchronised nod, like that dog you see in the back of some cars.

'Good,' Ferguson repeated, 'now, please see yourselves out. I have work to do and have no more time to spend on you useless mongrels.'

The four friends shuffled out of the room where they were met by four of the in-house security men. These men then directed them out the front door where the four drivers were waiting by the four BMW's, to take them home.

The journey home was less stressful than the ride there had been, mostly because every mile took them further away from Ferguson and his overindulgent life. Liam, his mind awash with worry, did not sleep.

A Sharp Intake of Breath

None of them had slept, that night. They had spent the rest of the evening in their own homes, apart from Liam who decided to visit his mother. She was getting steadily worse by the day. The doctors warned him that it was unlikely she would last the week. Liam went numb when he received this news. His mother was unable to do anything for herself, now. She was wired up, bagged up and had so many tubes in her that she looked like a Sebastien Wierinck installation.

Liam could not imagine life without his mother. To be more honest, he could imagine it but he did not like the idea one little bit. The way life was going at the present, with his mother hospitalised, he could not hope that things would be any easier once she passed over to the next world; he largely believed that it would get a lot tougher. To make matters more unbearable, he still had no idea how they were to get out from under Ferguson's sturdy thumb.

Ferguson had said that they now owed him. That did not sound good to Liam. Working for the man was bad enough but when you owed him a favour then he then held a much tighter grip on you. Liam and the other three had done everything that was asked of them and had, for the most part, been successful at what they did. However, every time they thought that they might be turning a corner, they got battered by someone or something, around the bend. Things just seemed to be getting worse and worse, as time passed on. First, they had stolen Ferguson's car, of all people; then they had been forced into dealing weed; after that was the grand theft auto; all before they bungled their attempt on the People's Palace. What Ferguson would ask of them next was a complete mystery.

At six in the evening, the group met up at Liam's mother's flat, soon to be Liam's, and waited for the inevitable arrival of Ron. They wished that they had any idea at all about what was planned for them but Ferguson had given no indications. They were completely in the dark and did not like it.

When seven o'clock chimed on the old carriage clock which sat on the mantlepiece, they all held their breaths as they waited. They did not wait long. Before even a minute had passed, they heard a knock on the door. Liam got up to answer it. When he returned, however, his face was white. The reason for this soon became apparent when Ron, followed by four lads in their mid-twenties, entered the room behind him. The lads were each carrying two large black holdalls, eight in total, one in each hand.

'Who are these guys?' Sparks asked, as politely as she could manage.

'These are your new supervisors,' Ron grinned. 'They have a good setup in the city but it is better off all round if we keep as much of our operation outside of Glasgow. We don't want to be getting involved in anything messy; a certain retired businessman's personal affairs, for one.'

Liam and the others all knew who Ron was referring to. Simon Miller was as close to being a Glasgow Godfather as anyone else had been since the days of Walter Norval and Arthur Thompson. He never gained such a standing as Norval or Thompson, no matter how frightening his reputation was, but he was close enough to their level to garner respect from anyone who knew the name. He was as much feared as he was esteemed. That went without saying. If Miller asked you to do something then that was what you did, no questions asked. *And you kept your mouth shut afterwards.*

Ferguson, who thought himself Lord of the Manor, was nowhere near this level of businessman and he could never have the gall to hope for anywhere near the same respect as Norval or Thompson held. Therefore, he chose to run his business out of the small town of Kilmarnock, south-west of the big city. He did not want to be attracting the attentions of those who might wish to close him down and shut him up (for good!). Ferguson feared Miller, as well he should. Miller may be retired but he was still nobody to mess with.

The older businessman now spent his time writing books. Liam had read a couple and, he had to admit, they were enticing and inciting. He had never imagined before,

250

what had really gone on gone down in that fair city during the nineties.

He had obviously heard of the ice-cream wars, and of the madmen who had gone round the city giving Chelsey smiles to children (*they were soon dealt with, quietly but effectively. This sort of thing was not approved of in in any circles*), but there was so much more that Liam had not known about.

Norval's daughter, for instance, had broken into the courthouses, one dark night, and set the place on fire, just so that she could destroy certain evidence against her beloved father. *Such brazenness*, Liam had thought, when he heard the story, as told by one Robert Jeffrey.

Ferguson, however, although he acted superior, was not on the same level. He was much, much further down the ladder and those above terrified him.

Which was why there were now four older boys setting up a weed processing workshop in Liam's mother's kitchen.

Ron had explained that, since Liam's mother was currently indisposed, it was a good time to, 'entreat entrance,' at his chamber door. Liam thought Ron had been reading too much Poe, for his liking, but he felt unable to decline Ron's non-request. Liam's opinion had no clout and never would.

When the four newcomers (Johnathan, Brian, Rogers and Frederick) had been introduced, Ron said his goodbyes and the four friends were left alone with their new supervisors, as Ron had called them.

This was less than ideal. No sooner were they all set up, than Liam, Sparks, Shug and Angus were thrown a black bin bag, each filled with different varieties of weed; *White Widow, Hindu Kush, Acapulco Gold* and, of course, the old favourite *Purple Haze*.

It was at this point that the four inexperienced youths were given a crash course in weed history whether they wished it or not.

White widow had been bred by a man who called himself Shanibaba. It had been told to Liam, once, that it was a cross between the indica and sativa strains. Liam had no reason to doubt this.

White widow had become one of the most popular hybrids on the open market, even though (or maybe because) it was so hard to find.

Hindu Kush, also derived from indica, has its origins in Pakistan. The newcomers had told the four friends that there was a range of mountains, there, which the weed was named after. It, too, was a fairly popular strain.

Acapulco Gold, on the other hand was a parent of the very first skunk weed and, therefore, ancestor to most hybrids across the globe. Skunk had become well sought after and so it had been used in the vast majority of hybrid attempts. It had a potent numbness to it which was desired by certain discerning ladies and gentlemen. Acapulco Gold is to cannabis as J.S. Bach is to classical music.

And let us not forget about Purple Haze, the newcomers had said, eventually. Coloured like its name would suggest, it was mostly down to Jimmy Hendrix that this particular strain was so greatly desired. Popular among creatives, this strain heightened the imagination and gave the patient a happy internal glow.

After the lesson was done, Liam was entrusted with the Kush while Sparks, Shug and Angus took the Widow, Gold and Haze, respectively.

They were told to weigh out ounces into smaller bags until they were halfway through their bin bag. Then, they were to swich to half ounces until they had but a quarter of the bag remaining. After that they were expected to weigh out quarter ounces until there was all but an eighth of the bag left. Then it was the turn of the three-point-five-gram eighths until one sixteenth of the original amount lay loose at the bottom of the bag. The rest of the weed was then to be weighed out into grams.

It took five hours of hard slog just to weigh out the ounces. By that point, everyone was exhausted and needed to sleep.

This they did.

Remaining in the flat, they all slept like never before, their brains numb from the repetitive actions.

When they awoke, they were allowed fifteen minutes to get themselves a cup of tea and some breakfast before they were all expected to begin again.

The day came and went but by the time ten o'clock PM came around, they were almost finished the three-point-five-gram eighths. With only the gram bags to complete, they had begun to feel a little better. They quickly ordered some food, before the chippy closed and ate in silence. As soon as they were done, they all went to their resting places (be it bed, couch or rug) and that was them till they repeated their operations, the next morning.

*

By the evening of the third day, they had managed to weigh out and bag up all four black bin bags. The four friends considered this to be quite an achievement. The newcomers, however, saw it more as an everyday occurrence. *Their operation must be huge,* Liam thought to himself as they ate their super. It had been explained to them that the weed would now be sent to certain individuals in Glasgow and Edinburgh. They would sell it on, mostly to students and old hippies, at a slightly higher price than they were expected to pay Ferguson. The stoners got stoned, the dealers got paid and Ferguson was able to distribute in the cities without worrying about upsetting people of a particular temperament.

Everyone was happy. Everyone, that is, except Liam, Sparks, Shug and Angus. To be honest, Angus was not too encumbered. They were afforded a certain amount to smoke themselves and so far, Angus had smoked all of his own allowance and half of Shug's. Shug, Sparks and Liam had preferred not to smoke while they were weighing out and so had managed to keep their personal stashes relatively untouched, in a way that Angus found himself unable to do.

With their task finalised and the separated parcels divided up between the six separate boroughs which Ferguson had been able to infiltrate, Liam imagined that the four newcomers would then leave. *This did not happen.*

For some time later, longer that Liam and the others dared to remember, Liam's mother's flat was used as an operational base for Ferguson's leading cannabis venture. What made the whole thing worse was that, six days after the newcomers had arrived, Liam's mother passed on.

Liam was grateful that he had managed to at least be there at the moment she left. It was purely by chance that she went on that particular night but he was with her at the end and that was what mattered.

Liam had not been in a good mood when he arrived back home, that evening. One of the newcomers made some kind of crass joke about the flat being up for grabs and Liam went for him. With fist and boot, Liam pounded on the twenty-year-old. The oppressed man could do nothing to stave off the maddened teenager, so he did all he could do; he curled up in a ball and tried, with all his might, to protect his most vital organs.

The other three newcomers eventually managed to pull Liam off the tormented man, who looked like he was about to cry. Liam had tried to resist and even managed to get another two boots into the man's side before he was wrestled to the ground. One of them even stamped on Liam's face, for good measure.

Liam still had that tell-tale bruise on his face when he attended the funeral. He wore dark glasses, of course, to try and hide the purple marks but he was sure that some of his mother's friends had noticed. One person certainly noticed.

'What the hell happened to you?' asked Tommy, as he pulled the glasses from Liam's face. A bruise, covering a quarter of the boy's face, was shown clear as day.

'Stop it,' Liam slighted, grabbing the glasses back from the old barman and pushing them back onto his face. 'I had a disagreement with a lamppost, that's all.'

'Is that a fact?' Tommy replied, not believing a word of it. 'Shaped like a boot, was it?'

Liam scowled. 'It's got nothing to do with you, anyway.' Liam rebuked the man.

'I'm sure your father...' Tommy began, but Liam was having none of it; not today.

'He can go and lie down there with my mother,' Liam shouted. 'He as good as put her on the track to an early grave, the day he left us. I don't care what he does or doesn't think.'

'Liam,' Tommy sighed, 'I think there's something you should know.'

Liam had had enough of conversation and said as much. 'Look, I can't be dealing with this, right now. I'm off home.'

'What about all the folks who want to give you're their regards?' asked Tommy, directing his hand at all the funeral guests.

'Them?' Liam scorned. 'I haven't seen any of them in years. They only chose to come once she was dead. Some friends, they were. I have nothing to say to any of them and nothing I wish to hear *from* them. I'll see you later.' With that, he walked off, in a huff and in the direction of the bus stop.

Love Thy Neighbour

It had taken forty-five minutes for the bus to arrive and, to make matters worse, the back seat was filled with ignorant ten-year-olds with sociopathic leanings. He wisely ignored them and avoided eye contact, taking a seat in the front row, right next to the doors. It was a short drive back and was a mere fifteen minutes before the bus came to a stop, a hundred yards from the entrance to what was now his flat.

As Liam stepped off and made his way towards the stairwell entrance, he was spotted by one of his elderly neighbours as she pinned her own children's newly cleaned school clothes to the communal line.

'Good afternoon, Liam,' she greeted in a kindly fashion. 'How's your mother doing? I haven't seen her in a while.'

Liam went from numb to being close to tears, in a matter of a second. 'She passed away, the other day, Mrs. McCormack,' Liam replied, as best he could. 'She never was well enough to come home again.'

'Oh, I am sorry to hear that,' Mrs. McCormack said, in a soft and honest voice. 'Do you need me to do anything? Happy to help in any way I can. All you need to do is ask.'

'That's very kind of you, Mrs. McCormack,' Liam replied, holding back the tears. 'I think I'm alright for the moment.'

'No problem. You just remember, anything at all, don't hesitate to chap on mine and Arthur's door. She was a good woman, your mother.'

Liam was grateful for the offer. 'Thank you, I'll bear that in mind.'

Just as Liam was heading off to his flat, Mrs. McCormack called after him. 'Oh,' she said, 'I've been hearing a lot of noise coming from your flat, over the last few days, and a lot of new faces coming and going. No other problems are there?'

'No Mrs. McCormack. I'm sorry about the noise. We'll keep it down from now on.'

'Okay then, dear. You know where I am if you want to talk.'

Liam thanked Mrs. McCormack again for her kindness and trotted back to his flat before she could detain him any further.

When Liam entered the flat, it was to the sound of Shug yelling at the top of his voice. 'If you come anywhere near her, again,' he was yelling, 'you'll be tasting rubber for a week.'

'I'd like to see you try,' one of the newcomers replied. 'A scrawny wee thing like you couldn't punch his way out of a paper bag.'

'We'll see about that, ya wee jobby,' cried Shug, slipping into the vernacular. 'Come here while I knock the shite out of you.'

The argument soon turned into a fight and the newcomer was quickly educated on the rights of woman, by a swift kick in the googlies and, once he dropped to the floor, an elbow to the top of the skull. This particular newcomer, three seconds into the fight, fell to the floor, unconscious.

The other three had good mind not to interfere this time. It had been hard enough to drag Liam away on the previous occasion and that was over a bad choice of repertoire. This time, however, they were bright enough to notice that Shug was in a not-so-blind rage and to interfere would be a terrible decision. Even though the newcomers were all a good eight to ten years older than the four young natives, they were not fighters. Shug's instable reaction to a simple comment regarding the loveliness of Spark's legs, was enough to make them pause.

Pulling their associate up off of the floor, they carried him through to the spare room and made him comfortable.

*

Half an hour later, after they had all calmed down, one of the newcomers came back into the room, taking great care to keep as far away from Shug as possible.

'We've received word from Big Ron that there's a large shipment coming in, this weekend. We all need to be ready to take receipt of our portion, as soon as it hits dry land. Can't have this kind of thing lying around the docks for too long.'

Liam did not need this. It had been a hard-enough time as it was without adding this to the list. He told them, in no uncertain terms, that they would have to explain it all properly the next day. He was going to his bed and was not to be disturbed. With one man still unconscious in the other room, nobody made any attempt to argue.

That night, Liam slept well but dreamed strange dreams that were gone from him as soon as he awoke. Dreams were often like that. They could be as clear as day while sleeping but entirely unmemorable after the fact. That is just the way life goes.

Hot Metal

It was explained to them, the next morning. Liam, Shug and Angus were to act as getaway drivers, each alongside one of the newcomers who would be riding shotgun. This was alright by Liam. He did not feel much like getting out of the car, anyway. It suited him perfectly to be in the driver's seat, patiently waiting for the moment where he would roll down the Troon docks, have the waiting dock workers load up the boot and then drive off, calmly to the drop-off point.

It was all so simple but Liam had an itch in the back of his brain, telling him that something was not right. He did not discover what that was until he parked on the dockside, engine running, observing the dock workers unload the unspecified cargo from the ship. The product was not in bags.

Instead, it was boxes they unpacked; crates even. They were around two and a half feet in length with the depth and height each being about twelve inches. A company mark Liam did not recognise was fire-branded on the side with the initials A.H. in the centre of it. To the right of said logo was the serial number marking, identifying the contents as *L24601-L24624*. What was also a little troubling was that the two men who were carrying the crates down the plank were bent at the knee and the back, as they strained to keep the package raised above the ground. It appeared to Liam that they were attempting to perform one of those Hungarian squat kick dances on the move. *Unlikely*, Liam thought but something was indeed not right.

'That's not weed, is it?' Liam asked the newcomer beside him.

The newcomer grinned. 'You're quick,' he remarked, sarcasm dripping off his tongue. 'No, it's not weed. This is something much more valuable.'

At this point, one of the two men who were carrying the crate, tripped and one end of the small crate hit the floor. Some of the contents dropped out and lay there, on the oily floor, glinting majestically in the moonlight.

Liam was stunned. 'Gold?' he asked, in awe.

'You just keep this to yourself,' the newcomer warned. 'The last thing we need is to attract he wrong kind of attention.'

'You don't have to tell me twice,' Liam assured. 'Who am I going to tell, anyway? It's not like anyone would believe me in any case.'

'You just better not,' he was warned.

When the dock workers had managed to shift all three crates of gold into the boot of the car, Liam set off with the newcomer in the passenger seat, giving Liam directions. Everything seemed to be going well, at first, but there was no time for congratulating themselves. No sooner had Liam exited the Troon docks and onto the main road, than lights started flashing, blue and red. Sirens pierced their ears as they became surrounded by police from every direction but one. This just happened to be dead ahead. Having come to a sudden stop, Liam looked to the newcomer for confirmation.

'*Hit it*,' was the instant answer.

Liam slipped back into first gear and pressed down hard on the accelerator, pulling off of the clutch at the same time. They took off. Liam was impressed. The car they had found for him was a matt-black Subaru Impreza with blackened rims. The car had been built for the single-track, dirt roads of the professional rally competitions, but it was just as good while wearing street tyres.

The Impreza shot off into the distance with the police barely able to keep up. If the roads had been empty and there were no people walking about then Liam could have raced away from the oncoming law and would never be seen again. As it was, he was hampered by other road users who he could not pass because of more vehicles coming towards them, on the opposite side of the road. Twice, he had to slam on the breaks; once to avoid crashing straight into an old lady and her shopping cart; and again, when a businessman, all his attention on his mobile telephone call, stepped straight out into the road, never caring to look where he was going. He simply looked up as Liam screeched to a halt, before him, and shook his head in dismay. *Cocky little shit*, Liam thought, bricking himself. *I could have killed him.*

They left the tiny town of Troon by the old Loans Road, heading north-east towards Dundonald. They were in and out of the small collection of houses in less than a minute When Liam glanced at the rearview mirror, the police were still hot on their tail. Joining the A759, Liam put his foot flat on the floor and hurried on, north through Gatehead and back into his hometown of Kilmarnock.

Now, things were different. This was Liam's patch and he knew the streets as well as anybody; better than the oncoming Trooninian police at any rate.

They entered by Dundonald Road and stayed true until they reached St Marnock's Street, where they took a sharp right. As they passed the police station on the corner,

Liam's unwanted passenger pushed himself through the sunroof opening and gave the local officers as many fingers as he could manage before they got across the river and out of sight.

Liam sighed at the newcomer. Here he was, on the run from the police and this numskull was his shotgun buddy. He could think of dozens of people he would rather have beside him. Actively giving the finger to unwitting police officers while carrying a load of dodgy gold in the back of the car was not wise.

At the end of the street, where the road turned only to the right, Liam made a quick decision. He threw the car down the Burns pedestrian precinct, to his left, in a mad hope that the police would think twice about doing the same. He was wrong and they all ended up, speeding precariously down the footpath at fifty miles an hour, fearfully witnessing the pleb and the affluent alike, as they dove wildly out of their way, into shops and alleys.

Changing over to the Portland Street footway, Liam headed true towards the main road. It was here that his plan went awry. As Liam threw the Impreza to the right, aiming down towards the old kirk, he swung too hard. The car tipped; turned and rolled across the road and ended up in the window display of the local home furnishing shop of Mason Murphy.

The pair lay there, still as a board. It was over. They were out of luck and in the jail. Having three crates of gold bars hiding in the trunk was not going to be an easy thing to explain. This was not how Liam had wanted his story to end but, in a lot of pain and slowly drifting off into dreamland, he was somewhat relieved. No longer would he be any use to Ferguson. He would have no need to do any more jobs or again see those bastards who took over his mother's flat.

Surely, from now on, things should go easier for him. Liam did not truly believe any of this but it was a nice thought, all the same.

Men Behaving Badly

Liam awoke in the hospital. He hurt all over and his brain seemed to be dancing a schottische, inside his skull. The good news was that he did not appear to have broken anything. He could still move his arms and legs; he was not attached to any tubes or wires; and, most importantly, he was not handcuffed to the bed.

Liam looked toward the doorway. Behind the glass, he could see the shadow of what looked like a police officer who faced away from the door, talking to what looked like a nurse. Between Liam and the door, lay a chair where his clothes had been folded and piled up. He carefully swung his legs over the side of the bed and sat up. Even this slow movement, sent his head spinning. There was no time, however, to give in to a body that was being bloody minded. He had to get out of there. If he delayed, he might miss his chance and then he would assuredly be in the jail before he knew it.

That was not an option. Whatever happened, there was no way Liam was about to let someone lock him up in what could only be described as a cupboard. That was no life, at all. Liam craved the fresh air, the ability to go wherever he wanted, whenever he wanted and for however long he wanted. He needed his freedom. He would not cope in the jail. He was not built for it.

Slowly lowering one foot to the floor, Liam assessed his situation. The pain was bad but he managed to stifle the scream that he so greatly desired. If he was careful, he could get enough weight on his legs to enable him to walk, painstakingly sluggishly out of the room. If he could also do it while the police officer was otherwise engaged, all the better.

Liam got dressed, eventually, and hobbled over to the door. Quietly, he pressed down on the handle and eased the door ajar. The officer hadn't heard it. Liam opened the door some more and looked around it. The police officer was in the middle of an amusing anecdote and would not notice his wayward ward.

Liam went. He did not look around, he did not stop. Liam did not have anything else on his mind but for getting out of the hospital and back to the flat. They would come looking for him there, later on, but before that happened, Liam would have time to pack a bag and leave for good. Go to Manchester or maybe Inverness. Both might be too close, still.

He could decide, later. At that moment in time, Liam's only desire was to get out of that place and go home.

But that was not to be. As Liam reached the pavement, with a mind to cross the road, he was grabbed by the neck and thrown into the back of a van. He did not see his kidnapper but the man's build seemed familiar.

'Damnit,' Liam yelled.

'Hush now, loon,' came a voice from the other side of the bag which had been pulled down over Liam's head. 'We'll no' be lang noo.'

Indeed, the journey was not long at all and when they eventually took the bag off of Liam's head, he saw that he was in that first room he visited while attending the Keys restaurant and Bar.

'Shite,' he reiterated.

He had been tied to the chair, again. This time, however, it was with rope. They had secured him with five loops around his chest, tied off, and five loops around each of his legs, also tied off. There was no way that Liam was ever going to be able to escape; not without a great deal of help. Yet, he knew in the very heart of himself that there was no help coming.

He sat there for about an hour, it was hard to tell. After that age had passed, the door opened and in walked Ron and Charlie. Ferguson was close behind them, as usual. Ferguson walked into the middle of the room and stared at Liam, calculating. Calculating what, Liam couldn't say. After what felt like another hour, Ferguson stopped his internal judgements of the boy and sat down on the chair, opposite.

'Well,' he said, softly, 'I must say, I have had many pets in my time but none of them ever laid such a big a shit on the rug, as you did, last night. What a fucking mess.' This was not the jovial, everything will work out fine, Ferguson that Liam had come to know. This was the pissed off gangster who wants his gold back.

'I will ask you this only once,' Ferguson continued. 'What did you tell the police?'

Liam shifted, uneasily in his binds. 'I never told them anything,' he replied.

'Come now,' Ferguson countered, 'you don't expect me to believe that they let you go, just for kindness sake. Do you think my head's buttoned up the back? *What* did you tell them?'

'Nothing, I promise,' Liam yelled. 'They didn't let me go. I escaped.'

Ron and Charlie laughed.

'Of course, you did,' Ferguson soothed, 'and, pray, how did you manage to get away from Scotland's finest?'

'They took me to the hospital,' Liam protested, 'and they didn't handcuff me to the bed. When the polis was talking to some pretty nurse, I legged it.'

Ferguson stared at him. 'I really wish I could believe you,' he said, 'but I need to know for sure. Ron and Charlie will look after you for a while and, before long, I *will* know the truth of it. Whether you'll survive to move on from this event, time will only tell.' He stood up and dusted himself down. Lighting a cigarette, he took a long draw and said goodbye, giving a significant nod to Ron before he went.

There was now only three of them in the room. Liam stared at the two hardened men, Ron and Charlie, as the young boy's heart pounded in his chest. Sweat ran down his face, in torrents, as he watched Charlie cross the room, towards him. The maniac smiled from ear to ear. As Liam considered

284

all possible outcomes, he found himself losing the power of his lungs, just at the thought of any of them coming to pass. None of the possibilities were good and he could not think of a single one, out-with wishing on a star, that would free him from this panic-inducing situation.

Charlie now stood directly in front of Liam. Ron had decided to stand at the back of the room with his arms folded across his chest. He seemed to have a concerned look on his face but Liam presumed it was just a trick of the light.

Charlie grabbed Liam by the chin with his left hand. 'I've been wanting to do this for such a long time,' he said. Charlies significant right hand closed into a fist and he sent it straight at the young boy's back teeth. Liam screamed in pain as his jaw near cracked from the force of Charlies muscular knuckles. He spat out a tooth. 'What the fuck?' he shouted, spitting blood out, after his tooth. 'I told you, I didn't talk.'

Charlie smiled some more. 'You heard the boss,' he said. 'We have to be sure.' With that, Charlie hit him, again but with his left this time.

Another tooth came out, followed by another pool of blood. 'How do you expect me to say anything if you keep hitting me in the jaw?' Liam argued. He was feeling a little woozy, already.

'That's a fair point,' Charlie replied, feigning niceties. 'Perhaps we should move on.' He walked over to the window and picked up a satchel that sat on the floor. Charlie took the bag over to the small table, the same one that had been in the room on Liam's initial visit. Opening the bag, Charlie retrieved a foot-long steel pipe with a leather grip tied around the base of one end. Liam recoiled at the thought of what Charlie was planning to do with it.

Charlie turned back to the bleeding boy. 'What did you tell them?' he asked.

'I told you...' Liam began.

Charlie did not wait for the end of the sentence. He raised the unclad end of the pipe, above his head and brought it down on top of Liam's right kneecap. The noise that came out of Liam was so incredible that anyone who didn't know that the room had more than ample sound proofing, would not believe the sound was unheard by any other living soul. He started to cry.

Charlie leaned down to Liam's ear. 'Oh, the poor wee baby,' Charlie lulled, mocking the boy. 'Have you gone peepee?'

Liam tried to headbutt his agitator in the face but Charlie was too quick. Liam just ended up with a case of whiplash to go along with his cracked jaw and battered kneecap.

'This isnae getting us onywhere,' Ron piped in. 'Gei the boy a rest, will ye. It's obvious he disnae ken a thing.'

'I'm doing my job, here,' Charlie thundered. 'What I want to know is, why are you not over here, getting *your* hands dirty?'

Ron glowered at his companion. 'I just dinnae think it's worth oor time. He didnae say onything to the polis. You ken that, just as I dae.'

'I dinnae ken a thing,' Charlie teased, '*yet.*' He turned back to Liam who was slouched in his chair, tears rolling from his eyes. 'Let's see, what's next?' he asked, rhetorically. He rummaged around in the satchel and pulled out something that Liam found truly abhorrent.

'Now, wait a minute,' he shouted, as Charlie came towards him with the pair of workman's pliers. 'Please, no. Don't you fucking dare.'

As quick as a cat, Charlie grabbed one of Liam's hands and held out the boy's middle finger. The masochist gripped onto Liam's unclipped fingernail with the pliers. He looked the poor boy in the eye. 'What did you tell them?' he asked again.

'Nothing, I swe...'

Charlie smiled, excitedly, as he ripped the nail out, in one clean pull. 'And you can scream the place down all you want,' Charlie added, 'this room is lead lined. You could be on the other side of that door and you wouldn't hear a dickie bird.'

Liam started crying. He really did look a mess and felt worse. His clothes were soaked with blood as his whole body twisted with pain.

'Now,' asked Charlie, 'any sudden enlightenment? A eureka moment, maybe?'

'Only that you're an arsehole,' Liam yelled back at him. 'I told you, I didn't say a thing to the police.'

Charlie grabbed him by the back of the head and wrenched it back. 'And *I* said, I don't believe you.'

Liam cried some more. He had never wondered before, how many tears someone could expel in one sitting. He was discovering that it was a great deal more than he could ever have imagined.

Charlie let go of Liam's hair and went back into his bag of tricks, one more time. On this occasion, he retrieved a large cloth and a bottle of water.

'Hold on a second,' Ron started. 'Dae ye no think that's gang a wee bitty tae far?'

'Na, you hold on. I'm doing what I was told to, which is a site more than I can say for you. Step back and leave me to it. This boy told them something, even if he doesn't remember yet. He's bound to have let something slip. So, don't butt in and don't try to stop me. If you do, I'll see to it that Mr Ferguson finds out about certain other goings on, if you know what I mean?'

Ron stood back, his hands raised in the air, portraying submission. 'Richt then,' he replied. 'Just mak sure ye dinnae kill him'

'Personally,' Charlie answered, as he turned towards Liam, again, 'I don't care, either way.' He walked around behind Liam, grabbed the back of the boy's chair and pulled it backwards with a sharp pull. Liam landed on the floor, on his back, still secured to the chair. Charlie knelt beside him. 'So,' he asked, 'what was it you told the police, again?'

'Nothi...' Liam started to say but Charlie was not about to wait for the answer. He laid the cloth onto Liam's face and pored the water straight onto it, suffocating the sixteen-year-old. He did this for only ten seconds but to Liam, it was like a lifetime. When Charlie stopped, it was as if Liam had come up from under the water, near dead from drowning. He coughed up some water as he also choked and spluttered everywhere.

Charlie grabbed the back of the chair again and lifted Liam back upright. 'Do we have something to say?' he asked, with a psychoneurotic slant.

'You're a fucking psychopath,' Liam gasped.

'Nope,' Charlie corrected, 'I'm just a man doing his job. Now, do you have anything to tell me before we move on?'

'What else could you possibly do to me?' Liam asked, regretting the words as soon as they were out of his mouth.

'Well, let me see,' Charlie said, 'I had been keeping this for a special occasion but as you inquired, I would so love for you to be the first to experience it. He dropped the cloth and empty water bottle back into the satchel and moved the whole bag down off the table. Walking across the room, motioning to Ron to move out of his way, he plucked a machine of some sorts from a cupboard. Ron's face dropped when he saw it and Liam started screaming obscenities when he came to realise what exactly it was.

Basically, in laymen's terms and not to put too fine a point on it, this was, to be sure, a car battery and a set of jump leads, one black and the other red. Nothing too complicated but enough to put the fear of God into anyone.

Charlie sat the items down on the table and walked around behind Liam again. He untied the boy's wrists and pulled them together, this time behind him, before tying them again. He then removed the binds that were wrapped around Liam's chest. Tearing off the Lewis Capaldi t-shirt that Liam had been wearing, Charlie left the boy naked from the waist up. Retrieving the remaining water, he poured the lot over Liam's head and chest.

'Now, again, before we start, what was it you told the police? You let something slip, I know it. Now what... was... it?'

'Look, you maniac,' Liam bellowed as the tears flooded and the blood matted, 'I didn't tell them a thing, never gave them a chance to ask. I woke up and ran.'

'Nope,' Charlie replied, 'don't believe it. Don't ever say I never gave you a chance.'

Charlie retrieved the jump leads from the table, one red and one black. After attaching one end of each of them to the battery, Charlie touched them together to test the premise. This was probably also for Liam's benefit. Charlie wanted him to be scared.

294

Liam was indeed pretty scared, had lost a great deal of blood and was in an incredible amount of pain but he was not about to let Charlie get the better of him. If he died, Liam thought, so be it but he was not going to let Charlie think that he had broken him.

Liam looked Charlie in the eyes, made his final decision and opened his big swollen mouth as he moved his head closer to the hulk of a man, whispering 'Bring it on, ya prick.'

Liam's body shook violently as the electricity passed from one nipple to the other as it took the shortest route between the two copper alligator clips. If Liam had been able to pay attention, he would also have suffered through the unpleasant odour of burning flesh.

The smell and the screaming did not worry Charlie, at all. Ron was still in his corner, wrestling with his conscience.

Charlie shocked the young teenager not just the once, not just twice, but three times, for five seconds at a time. Liam felt close to the end, each and every time and was praying, once again, that it would all end. He just wanted it all to stop. If that meant Charlie finishing him off, then Liam would be fine with that.

When Charlie lifted the jump lead away from Liam's nipples for the third time, he went to ask Liam his one question, again. He was however distracted, by someone bursting into the room. It was the lone security guard.

'Quick,' he stammered. 'Keys has been compromised. We have to get out now. Mr Ferguson's ordered an immediate Peshtigo. He said you'd know what that meant.'

Ron and Charlie did indeed know what it meant. Ron looked over to Liam, desperation in his face.

Charlie, pressed a hand on the north-eastern man's chest, saying, 'You go and find the boss. I'll deal with this.'

Ron looked unsure but left the room, anyway.

It was just Liam and Charlie, now. Charlie walked over to Liam and knelt in front of him. 'Well,' he said, 'it looks like this is the end of our interview. I'm sorry but we won't be meeting again. Me because I'm thinking of heading off to the sunny shores of Spain, for a while, and you because you'll be dead.' He grabbed the jump leads from where he had carefully placed them and held one to each of Liam's temples. The boy shook and burned and Charlie did not stop until a clear thirty seconds had passed. When he stopped, Liam was hunched over, unmoving. Charlie held a finger to his neck, searching for the faintest pulse. There wasn't one that he could find. He held a hand in front of the boy's face; no breath. When Charlie was finally confident that Liam was indeed dead, he lit a cigarette, took a few draws, to calm himself, and then tossed it into a basket of papers which sat in the corner of the room, next to a long curtain. As the room started to burn, Charlie backed away, spraying Liam, the walls of the room and corridor beyond with lighter fuel.

This had been planned out, years before and now it was time. The Keys was to have a little accident. Any evidence against them would be destroyed, Ferguson would collect on the insurance and they would start again, exactly where they left off, with a brand-new property. All right and proper.

Doctor in the House

...but that was then.

Liam left both the mortuary and the half-naked trainee doctor behind him, as he hobbled away from the Crosshouse University Hospital. He was in one hell of a state. Thankfully, the trainee doctor's coat sported a high collar. He also had the fortitude to have worn a flat cap, that morning. After stealing it from the student, Liam was able to tip it downwards in order to cast his face into shadow. Even with all this camouflage, he got some funny looks from people on the street.

Liam staggered along until he came to a bus stop. Here, he was able to catch a ride to the only place he could think of going. He only had to wait five minutes before the right bus arrived. When he stepped up onto the carriage, the driver looked him up and down. Liam's apparel and sickly demeanour, led the driver to assume that the boy was a misfit medical student who had been out all night, drinking. Liam showed him the bus pass which he had found in the trainee doctor's coat pocket, and he was waved on.

Liam sat at the back of the bus. He was in no mood to have anyone behind him. He wanted to have eyes on everyone and everything. He was far from being out of the woods, yet and the police would surely be looking for him. Ferguson would, too if he had even an inkling that Liam was still alive. He would want to finish the job. Liam had to keep low to the ground, so to speak. If he was spotted by anyone who knew him, he would be in more trouble than he'd ever been in his lifetime.

When he saw his stop coming up, Liam pressed the red button and a short ring rang out to let the driver know that he wanted to alight. His mind rolled and fizzed as he limped and stumbled his way, along the road. When he finally managed to get to where he needed to be, he paused, quickly placing a hand on the wall, to brace himself. His heart was pounding and his knee was on fire. Everything else was simply numb. Liam tried to hold his weight, again. This did not work and he dropped to the floor losing consciousness; yet not before he managed to cry out in pain.

Only When I laugh

Liam awoke. It was not quick. Light did not flash. His brain did not go ping. This was more sluggish. It was as if the darkness which succeeded his dreams, simply began to drift away and the room in which he then found himself, came slowly and steadily into focus. When he could see well enough to peruse his surroundings, he was more than pleased that above him were not the crumbling council ceiling tiles of a hospital ward.

More so, it was a place he recognised and, as it happened, the place he had intended to be. That being said, Liam still let out an uncontrolled shudder when he observed the old lacklustre but reassuringly familiar back room of the Ginger Nightcap.

Liam remembered it from his childhood. He had used to play back there whenever his father was having a business meeting. What business he might have needed to do in a bar, Liam never knew. He had never thought about it, if he were telling the truth. There were no whys or wherefores, back then. That was just how things were. They did not need explaining.

Turning his head, to look to the back door, he considered the possibility that coming to that place had been a misguided thought. Although he was still in a great deal of pain, he found that he could bend his knee so it wasn't as badly damaged as he had previously thought. Maybe, he could still run away, somewhere. The Western Isles were looking more promising, every day. If he could escape and find his way up the A9, without anyone catching on, maybe he could start a new and better life where nobody knew who he was.

'I hope you're not thinking about bolting, already,' said a voice from out of the darkness.

Liam moved his sights from the door to the far corner of the room. Cameron Buchanan, Liam's father, had been sitting in the corner, reading by the window. He laid the book down on a side table. 'You're in quite a state,' he informed Liam. 'Whoever did this to you, knew what they were doing.'

'Yeah,' Liam replied, 'well, let's just say that there's a man out there who'll be pretty annoyed if he discovers I'm still alive.' Liam sat himself up. 'Look,' he continued, softer than before, 'I'm not here looking for help. All I need is a place to lay low and recuperate, before I can decide what I'm going to do, next.'

And what is that?' his father asked.

'North maybe,' Liam suggested, 'or possibly south. I haven't decided, yet.'

'Good plan,' his father ridiculed. 'Why don't you tell me what happened?'

Liam peered at his father. He had an honest look about him, as if he truly wanted to know.

'It's a long story,' Liam attempted.

'I'm not going anywhere.'

Liam sighed and gave in. He told his father about stealing Ferguson's car; how he had forced them to sell weed in Glasgow; about how they had to rob three supercars from a ship in Troon; of the time they had failed to break into the People's Palace; and all about the boot full of gold bars. He told him about how Ferguson believed Liam had blabbed to the police and had told Charlie to torture the apparent information out of him; about all the things that that evil man had done; and about how he had left Liam for dead.

All through Liam's story, his father listened with intent. Eventually, when Liam had recounted all he could remember, his father spoke. 'Okay. Now we have something to work with.'

Liam looked blank. 'What?' he asked.

'I know Willie Ferguson and I believe that I can have a quiet word with him on this matter.'

'You might think that you know him,' Liam protested, 'but he's much worse than that. He'd strangle a baby... in a packed-out church... on easter Sunday, if he thought it would make him some money.'

'I know the type,' his father agreed. 'I'll have a wee word with him all the same.' He stood up as if to leave.

Liam protested again, this time wholeheartedly. 'Look, I don't want your help. I don't want anything from you. You were never there before and I managed to survive. I don't need you sticking your nose into my business, now. Just let me crash here tonight and I'll be out of your hair by morning.'

'Are you quite finished?' his father asked. 'I am your father and always will be. I may not have been able to raise you, these past years, but I still provided for you. I made sure that your mother never needed to work; paid to have a roof kept over your head; put food on your table. I did everything I could. It wasn't my decision to leave.'

Liam spun his head towards his father, his face going red with anger. 'Don't you dare try and blame it all on my mother. She was the best woman I knew. You couldn't hold a candle to her.'

His father looked like he was about to say something, then stopped. He turned, smartly and opened the door to the bar.

Walking through it, he held his head low, shaking his head.

Father, Dear Father

Liam lay where he was, until he felt able to move without being sick. When he felt able. he sat up and then stood up. Testing his weight on his leg, his knee, which had been bandaged with some degree of professionalism, seemed stronger than the previous evening. He limped over to a shelf where lay a couple of dozen open bottles of spirits. This was where all the bottles went when the brand was no longer sold under that roof. This could come about for a few reasons, the main one being a disagreement with a certain brewery or supplier; or maybe Cameron Buchanan simply felt like a change.

Liam chose a bottle of White Dog Whisky and sad down on a chair by the desk. It was a clear whisky, which is what drew Liam to it. He had never seen such a thing before.

To him whisky should be golden, moonshine was clear. Made from corn, rye and malted barley, it was more of a bourbon than a whisky. Liam read on the back where it said, 'Bottled before it meets the barrel...'. Liam did not have to read any further. This was going to be rough. Right at that point, though, he did not honestly care. He was not sure how long he was going to be able to survive, out there, on his own. A spot of the world's worst whisky might just give him the jolt he needed to at least get a head start.

He threw back a mouthful and regretted it, instantly. The clear liquid burned Liam's mouth, tongue, throat and kidneys alike. His kidneys would be crying out for mercy as soon as they discovered for themselves what Liam had just done. It truly was the nastiest, most repulsive whisky, ever.

Liam looked at the bottle which had only ever had one other shot served from it before and shrugged. He threw back another mouthful and winced again. It tasted like crap and that 'swallowing razorblades' feeling was not pleasant, in the least. Nevertheless, it was numbing some of his pain.

As Liam went for a third helping, a hand grabbed the bottle out of the young boy's hand. 'What do you think you are doing,' came the voice of Tommy the barman.

Liam stared at the old man. 'I can drink if I like,' he smart-mouthed.

'Maybe out there,' replied Tommy, pointing to the outside world, 'but in here,' he pointed at the floor, 'in here, we only drink the best.' Tommy smiled at Liam. 'Put that crap down and come through to the bar. I'll fix you a proper drink. I know you're not quite of age, yet, but I've just closed up for the day and this is your father's bar, so I won't be selling you anything. Only a couple, mind. I don't want your father coming back and seeing you passed out on the floor for any other reason than that beating, you just got.'

Liam winced at the remembrance of being tortured. It would be a long time before he was going to be able to sleep a whole night through, again. *Maybe I could get some Valium?* he thought to himself. *That might help.*

It occurred to him that Tommy had said something about his father. 'I don't care what he thinks,' Liam replied. 'He's never been there for me before and I don't want him thinking he can start now, just because mum's gone.'

Tommy placed two glasses on the bar and poured from a bottle of twelve-year-old Balvenie Doublewood. This was more like it. A Balvenie was always nice but the Doublewood Twelve was something

312

glorious. It had been named as a Doublewood very simply because it spent time maturing in not just one barrel but two, the second being an old sherry butt. This gave the Doublewood a very pleasant aftertaste. As Liam sipped on it, he let the pleasant warmth of the golden liquid flow through his whole body. In a couple of hours, he would pee it all out again but wasn't that why they called it *'renting a whisky'* and not *'buying one'*? For the moment, though, Liam enjoyed the friendly glow that warmed him from the chest out.

After allowing Liam a few minutes of peace, Tommy cleared his throat. 'There's something you need to know,' he said.

'Don't,' Liam cautioned.

'You shouldn't really be hearing this from me but it's time you knew the truth about what happened, all those years ago.'

'I don't *want* to hear it,'

'Well, you're going to,' Tommy replied. 'I can't stand by any longer.' He poured another couple of healthy measures into his and Liam's glasses. 'Look, your father didn't just up and leave. Your mother told him to go.'

Liam scoffed.

'Things were different, back then,' Tommy continued. 'At the time, your father was involved in the business of a certain gentleman. I believe you know him?'

Liam looked up from the glass he had been studying. 'What? Ferguson?'

Tommy sighed. 'Indeed. Your father was an up and coming member and Ferguson even went so far as to name him as his successor.'

This was all news to Liam. Obviously, looking back on it, he never rightly knew what his father had done for a living and it could very easily be such as Tommy had posed.

'So,' Tommy went on, 'when your father decided that it was time to quit the game, Ferguson wasn't best pleased.'

'I'll bet he wasn't,' Liam replied, forgetting his disinterest.

'Ferguson tried to kill your father, on the spot, but he missed by an inch. Your father escaped and Ferguson sent his men after him. I believe you know Ronald Gove?'

Liam nodded, emphatically. 'Oh, yeah,' he said. 'I know him, right enough.'

'Thanks be to God,' Tommy persisted, 'Ronald had always respected your father and so the three of us cooked up a plan. Ronald would tell Ferguson that he had finished the job and dumped your father's body in the Irvine river; far enough away from Kilmarnock to keep curious eyes away from them. Your father was then to disappear for a while. Once everything calmed down, your father planned to come back again, this time with another identity, paired with a spot of plastic surgery.'

'So, what happened, then,' Liam asked. 'Did he just decide he had a better life without us?'

'You watch your lip,' scolded Tommy. 'Your father loves you as much today as he did when you came into this world; that is to say, more than himself. The reason he wanted to leave in the first place was to give more time to you and your mother. He had grown tired of the game and felt that, if you were to have any chance at a normal life then he would have to break all ties to Ferguson and his cronies.'

'He did all that, for me?' Liam was shocked.

'Indeed, he did. Everything he's ever done was for you and your mother. When he told your mother of Ronald's plan, he wanted to take you both with him. Your mother, however, said she wasn't about to take an eight-year-old boy off to a life on the road. She told him that, if he were serious about going through with the plan, he would have to go it alone. Only after she promised to wait for him, did he agree. After that, Ronald and your father made a grand show of knocking lumps out of each other. Ronald was to throw your father onto the street whence your father would run away. The idea was that Ronald would be seen to chase your father down the street and they would both vanish in the crowd.'

'So, what went wrong,' Liam inquired. 'I assume, something did?'

'It did,' Tommy verified. 'Charlie.'

'Charlie?' Liam had almost put that bastard out of his thoughts. 'What did he do?'

'He had followed Ronald, to help him give chase. He had no idea about the plan. Neither your father nor Ronald trusted him as far as they could throw him. Somehow, Charlie got to your father before he could make his escape. After a *one shank shuffle*, Charlie slipped that shank into your father's side. If the police hadn't turned up at the right time, he surely would have finished the job.'

'That was convenient,' Liam scowled.

'Indeed, it was,' Tommy agreed. 'Ronald is a quick thinker, at times and when he saw Charlie and your father pounding into each other, he did the only thing he could think of, short of killing Charlie. He called the cops.'

'So, they arrested Charlie for G.B.H.?' Liam deduced.

'Not quite,' said Tommy. 'They both got arrested on a count of disturbing the peace, spent the night in the cells and were released the next day. Thankfully, your father was let out a few hours before Charlie. That gave him time to get home to see you and your mother before he went on the lamb.'

'I remember that day,' Liam sighed. 'My mother was in tears.'

'And now you know why,' said Tommy. 'She loved your father till the end, as he did her. He was even there at her passing, looking in from the corridor to your rear. He says she looked him straight in the eyes that she knew so well, smiled and went.'

Liam's heart twanged a little. 'So why did he never come back, then,' Liam asked, in a last ditched attempt to lay blame at his father's feet, 'like he planned?'

'At first,' Tommy replied, 'it was safer for him to stay away from you both. He wanted to wait until he was sure that nobody would recognise him when he returned; hence why he grew the beard and shaved his head. When that time came, you had come to hate your father, so much so that he couldn't see any way of returning to the life that he had been dreaming of, for so long.'

Guilt started to rise up in Liam's chest as the resentment evaporated.

'He's been looking for a way back in for all these years,' Tommy added. 'Unfortunately, he never found one.'

This was more than Liam could take. In his pain, his anguish and his new-found understanding, he broke down in tears, unable to hold back the strain that had befallen him.

Tommy patted the boy on his arm and poured him another drink. 'That's it, lad,' he said. 'Let it all out.'

Still Game

After his talk with Tommy, Liam found his father, who had been down in the cellar, stock checking. The pair of them sat down there, in the damp room and talked for nearly two hours. Liam spoke of what had been going on with him over the last six months and his father went into more detail about what happened when Liam was eight.

After that cleansing conversation, they both made their way upstairs again. Liam was sat through in the back room with a bottle of coke. His father sat at the desk and made a few phone calls.

Liam had finally accepted his father's input on his problems, although he could not see how this would change his prospects. His father used to work for Ferguson, that was fair enough, but he knew what it was like to try and squirm your way out from under that man's wing. What did he really think he could do to help?

Liam listened as his father phoned round some of his friends, associates, call them what you will. The way his father spoke on the phone, Liam might have thought he was going to war. His sentences were short and his words were precise. There was no unrequired language. They answered, he said his piece, they both hung up. No single conversation, if you could even call them conversations, lasted more than ten seconds. This is why you do not get many female gangsters. It is not that they are less capable, which is certainly not true; and it is definitely not because they're less inclined; it's because they have difficulty understanding the concept of a brief telephone call.

After Cameron had completed his task, Tommy joined them. He had cleaned down the bar and locked the front doors, dropping the mandatory iron shutters, in front of the stained-glass windows. Tommy also brought a bottle of ten-year-old Jura with him. Cameron had insisted that Liam refrained from drinking any more of the golden water of life. Therefore, Tommy had pulled through a case of irn-bru, as well.

Liam, a little resentfully, opened a bottle of the ginger pop and took a sip. 'So,' he said, conversationally, 'who were all those guys you were phoning, earlier?'

'Friends of mine,' Cameron replied. 'Ones that don't play well with Ferguson, selected specially. Each one of them has a stake in this.'

Liam did not know what his father meant by this but decided not to press the matter. 'And what is it that you expect to come of it?' he asked. Liam was pretty depressed as it was and still had half a mind to run off to the Highlands and live off the land.

'Son,' Cameron replied, 'that man ordered you to be tortured. There is no way on God's green earth that I'm going to let that stand. You are my son. I plan on reigning down on him from a great height. He won't see us coming and won't be able to stop us when we do.'

'Is that strictly necessary?' Liam asked. 'I'm not looking to make things worse. What if it all goes wrong? He'll go nuts.'

'It won't go wrong,' Tommy piped in. 'This has been planned for a long time.'

Cameron nodded. 'Indeed. And now is the time to act. He's gone too far, this time. This week... *he... is... done.*' The growl that emitted from his father, when he said those last words, gave Liam the chills.

So, who *are* these guys, then, specifically?' Liam asked, hoping for a little more information on these mysterious gentlemen.

'You'll be able to see for yourself in a moment,' Tommy replied, who had been studying a group of monitors. 'That's them arriving, now.'

No sooner had the words left Tommy's lips than there was a rhythmical chap on the door. Tommy answered it and allowed entry to four octogenarians who looked like they'd been through both world wars.

Liam looked at his father and Tommy, raising one eyebrow in disbelief.

Liam's father smiled, knowingly. 'Welcome, gentlemen,' he said, 'glad you could all make it.' He directed them through to the bar where they took up residence around two tables which had been pushed together for this very purpose. 'I think we should do some introductions before we go any further,' Cameron continued. He pointed around the room. 'Everyone, this is my son, Liam. He's in a bit of trouble with a certain gentleman whom we are all acquainted.' He pointed at the man, sat next to his son. 'Liam, this is the Badger. Not that great in a fight, even back in the day, but he'll squirrel through any hole you can find. Triple jointed, isn't it, Badger?'

'Aye,' Badger confirmed, 'I am that.'

'And this,' Cameron went on, moving on to the next man, 'is Baloo. He can lift a man by the neck, with one hand, and crush a man's ribs just by giving him a hug.'

Liam could believe it. Baloo was a large man of great girth. Liam certainly wouldn't stand a chance with the man, if he got a grip on the young boy.

'Next,' Cameron continued, 'is Louis. He's a man with certain useful connections. Then next to him, you have Charlie's predecessor, Sparks. He can work magic with anything electrical from electronic sensors to an electric drill; only to be used in exceptional circumstances, of course.'

Liam paused the conversation. 'I have a friend who's also called Sparks,' he said, slowly.

'That'll be young Georgia, my granddaughter.'

'Your granddaughter?' Liam gasped. 'Really?'

'Indeed,' Cameron confirmed. 'In fact, The Badger and Baloo are also grandfathers to your other two friends.'

'What? Shug and Angus?'

'Indeed,' the Badger replied. 'Hugo is our Linda's eldest and Angus is Baloo's youngest's, middle child. Sid and Mary's kid, isn't it?' He looked to Baloo for confirmation. Baloo nodded.

'And what about you?' Liam asked of Louis.

'Oh,' Louis grinned, 'I'm just in this for the pleasure of sticking it to that self-righteous bastard, Ferguson. His comeuppance has been a long time coming and no mistake.'

Cameron gave a little cough. 'Erm,' he said, 'Louis, here, used to play for the other side.'

'He means the police,' Louis clarified. 'I got as far as Chief Inspector before they went and retired me. Still felt like I had more to give, you know?'

Liam looked at him, then to his father and back to Louis, again. This was information he did not expect.

Louis continued in his remembrance. 'I spent years trying to find a way to catch that bastard. Most of my career was dedicated to it. I managed to get a few of his lieutenants, from time to time, but it was never enough to put a decent enough dent in his operation. I'm hoping that, this weekend, that will change, somewhat.'

Liam considered all this new knowledge. It was a lot to take in, especially since he was still quite a way from recovering from his past ordeal. He eventually decided that it did not matter who these men were, only if they could really pull of whatever it was that they were planning.

'So,' Liam said, to the room in general, 'what is it that you are all planning to do to Ferguson and, most importantly, how are you going to make sure that there's no retribution?'

'I have an idea,' Cameron answered, happily.

The Office

For three days, the men worked out of Cameron's back office. They made plans; they worked out the schedules for everyone involved; they allocated jobs; they worked out a list of requirements; and they made sure that everyone knew exactly what they were supposed to be doing.

At the end of the third day, Liam's father came to him and said that he had invited some friends around. When the back doors opened and in walked Sparks, Shug and Angus, Liam had to admit that he was happy but a little surprised.

'You didn't think we were going to let you take on Ferguson alone, did you?' Sparks announced.

'I didn't want to put you guys in any more danger. Anyway,' he added, 'I wasn't going to be alone.'

330

'Yes,' Sparks replied, giving her wayward grandfather a furrowed brow, 'I know. Granny's been beside herself. He told her he was going down the allotment.'

'And what kind of a nickname is Badger?' Shug asked his own grandfather.

'It's done me alright, these last sixty-five years,' Badger replied.

At this point, everyone looked expectantly at Angus who merly stood on the spot, staring blankly at his petulant grandfather.

'What about you, boy?' Baloo asked. 'Have you not got anything to say?'

'No, sir,' Angus replied, softly.

Liam was surprised at Angus' reaction. He was not, as a rule, what you might call a polite young boy. To see this reaction to the voice of authority, someone whom Angus actually respected and obeyed, was strange.

'Young Aonghas[7], here, and I had a wee chat, last night,' Baloo went on. It was the first time that Liam had heard him speak and his thick Hebridean accent was a bit of a surprise. 'He has explained everything, even the parts regarding his foolishness, and he has promised me that such things will not happen again. Isn't that right, Aonghas?'

Angus nodded but said nothing.

'Good boy,' Baloo praised. 'Now, wasn't there something you wanted to say to your friends?'

Angus hung his head in shame. *'Sorry,'* he mumbled.

'I didn't quite catch that,' Baloo growled.

Angus winced. 'Sorry I got stoned and got us all nicked,' he recited, as if he had been compelled to learn the words.

---

[7] Scottish Gaelic word for Angus.

332

'Okay then,' Liam replied, still shocked at this servile performance from his usually outspoken friend. He looked round at Shug and Sparks.

They simply shrugged their shoulders in disbelief, saying, 'Fine then, us too.'

The deed done, they all started to breathe normally again. The four friends then gathered around the four older gentlemen, Tommy and Cameron. The plan was explained to them, in full. Nothing was left out. Cameron had said that, if everyone knew what everyone else was supposed to be doing, they could create changes in the plan along the way, without too much of a fuss. They would not have any time for long-winded explanations.

With everyone knowing what was to be done. Liam's father suggested that they all take the rest of the night to spend with their families. He did not have to say that it might be the last chance they would have. Although they had planned it well; and even though they were confident that they would come out of it, not just successfully but in glory; and even though they would have the element of surprise, there was always that small chance that something might go wrong. Someone could get injured or even die. Nothing was ever undeniable, in life. Hindsight may be twenty-twenty but foresight is blind.

Everyone filed off, after that. When Liam was alone in the back room with his father and Tommy, once more, he relaxed a little. Telling them that he was tired, Liam made his way up the stairs to the adjoining flat which came with the pub. There, his father had set him up with a room. It was a nice room and comfortable. Liam suspected, however, that most everything in there had been bought recently, just for him. One of the pillowcases still had the tags on it. He even found, on the first night, one of those small plastic clips they use to stop bedding from unfolding in the shop. Liam appreciated the effort.

He slipped off to sleep with ease, that night and dreamed, once again, of train tracks and opera masques.

To the Manor Born

Liam awoke at four in the morning. He did not know why. Usually, he could sleep and sleep but, for some reason or another, he was wide awake and itching to do something. He had been stuck in the Ginger Nightcap for a few days and the claustrophobia was kicking in. He needed to get out for a while.

Checking that his father was asleep, Liam crept down the stairs and stood in the back room as he put on his jacket and gloves. While there, he noticed a box that was sat on the table. When he looked inside, it was the masks they had used for the waterfront robbery, four months back. Liam pulled out the white one that he had used, that day. It felt lighter, now. Maybe it was something to do with having been through so much since that day. Maybe the fact that they had

336

experienced all that they had, had made them stronger of mind. If Liam were being honest, he could barely remember that young, naïve boy he used to be.

Liam slipped the mask into his pocket and left by the back door. As he walked, he found that the exercise was helping to ease the stiffness in his knee. It was still not perfect but much better than when he had first woken up in the morgue. He wandered, aimlessly, for some time, as he enjoyed the peace and quiet that came with such an early hour of the morning. It was so early, in fact, that even the bakers were only just switching on the lights in their back shops and the postmen were barely opening their eyes.

Liam walked, not with any particular destination in mind; selecting a course of action only when he reached a crossroads. He did this for about an hour and soon found that he was passing the new charging stations on the London Road. The idea of electric cars was not something that Liam knew much about. He had heard Sparks saying, once, that it was a good idea in theory but if any kind of popularity was going to be achieved for the general public and not just those who could afford to have self-charging outlets in their own home, more public chargers would have to be accessible, all up and down the country. At present, most of them were only in the cities. Another issue was that electric cars could generally only travel around one hundred and forty miles before you had to recharge. There were a few exceptions to this rule but the ones that could go longer distances were more than the average person could afford. The other main issue was that when you did need to recharge, it could take anywhere from one to fourteen hours to achieve this. Sparks had been quite vocal about it all. Her dream car was the *Tesla Model S* but, at one hundred and thirty thousand pounds sterling for the *Tri Motor All-Wheel Drive* (eighty thousand for the basic model), it was more than she would ever be able to afford in her lifetime.

As Liam continued up the road, he came to a point where the street changed from the London Road to Main. Here, a railway bridge crossed over the street. At that time in the morning, trains were few and far between. The ones carrying cargo had mostly gone where they were going and the ones that were to carry passengers to their individual workplaces had not yet begun to roll out for that day. Liam decided to hop on up and take a walk down the line, something that he had not done in some time.

Liam made his way south for only a short while, until he reached the point where the railway line crossed the Irvine River, on its way out of town. This part of the line was not used much, not leading anywhere and with no stops between there and the town. It was mostly used for temporary parking of carriages and turning, this made it one of the most peaceful sections of line on the South-west coast.

When Liam reached the bridge, he sat down on the line and stared back in the direction he had just come. He had a lot on his mind and being out in the fresh air with nobody looking to him for anything, he found a kind of peace. As he rested, cross-legged on the ribbed boards that secured the line to the bridge, he pulled a spliff out of his inside pocket and lit it, sending a puff of smoke out into the world as he drew in and exhaled the sweet vapours.

Liam continued to stare down the empty line. He was tired and sore and was still not sure if their plan, which they had been working on over the last few days, would work or if they would simply go down in a blaze of... if not glory then napalm, metaphorically, at least. Ferguson was a tough nut to crack and, even with all the help that they now had, Liam found it difficult to see how things could work out, in a way that would allow them to get back to a reasonably normal life.

Pulling the mask from out of his pocket, he stared at it. He had not thought much about it since they had worn them for that first robbery. Now, as he held it in his hands, he felt a strange sense of fate. The only other time he had seen it was when he had been forced to work for Ferguson. Now, the final time he planned to wear it, it would be to take the old gangster down, hopefully for good.

Liam breathed and drew in his final draw of the sweet smoke. Seeing the sun rise to the east, he looked at his watch. Six o'clock. He would have to be getting back before anyone noticed he was gone and started to worry. He had enjoyed his walk and the fresh air had done him good. It had been a long time since he had found himself able to relax, like that. Life had become so busy and complicated that he rarely found time to get a shut-eye, let alone properly relax in his own mind with nobody else around to disrupt his moment of calm.

When he arrived back at the Ginger Nightcap, the only other person who was up and moving was Tommy who had wanted to clean out the beer pipes before the day begun because, as he said, 'There's no point putting off the everyday responsibilities that need done, just because you currently have other things on your mind.' The pumps needed cleaning and so Tommy made sure that they were cleaned. Liam helped his aging friend and before they knew it, they were finished and eating the obligatory fried breakfast before anyone else appeared. This consisted of two sausages, four rashers of bacon, a couple of fried eggs, mushrooms, baked tomato, fried bread, two tattie scones, two hash-browns, a large portion of baked beans, a side of chips and a couple of pork chops which Tommy had found in the fridge. 'They need eating up,' he had said, as he dropped a couple of slices of toast down in front of the hungry boy, 'and we may as well be the ones to have them.'

As the others trickled in, two-by-two, Tommy made bacon rolls available, as well as a good strong mug of tea, each. It was always important, when going out on a job, to make sure that you were well fed, watered and relieved of all bladder pressure. The last thing you wanted was to have to go for a pee, midway.

Once breakfast was consumed, the group began to go through the plan, one last time. As they did, Cameron, along with the three grandfathers and Louis, had a few choice words to say about Ferguson. When he heard his father speak, like that, he could tell the differences between him and Ferguson quite clearly. One difference was that Ferguson was born to money and had grown up in a stately home, north of Falkirk town. Liam's father, on the other hand, had been brought up in an elderly housing estate, run by the local council. While Ferguson dined on bulls testicles and bird nest soup, Liam's father imagined culinary heights as being a breaded fish supper with a side of pickled egg. Also, Ferguson was sent to the most expensive public school around, where he patiently learned debating and honed his leadership skills. Liam's father had been trained on the streets and learned quickly to dodge the first punch and land the second.

The two men could not be more different; the learned, William S. Ferguson and the incorrigible, Cameron W. Buchanan. When it came down to it, these differences would be everything. Whoever was on top, once everything went down, would owe their success to their own upbringing. Liam suspected that Ferguson, with all his learning, was too confident for his own good. He hoped and prayed that, if it came to blows, his father would come out on top.

Come what may, they had but a short time to make sure that they were ready for whatever the night might throw at them. They went over everything twice and then a third time, to make sure Angus was in no doubt as to what was expected of him.

Angus made no comment and spoke very rarely which was very unlike him. The influence of his grandfather certainly appeared to be doing the boy some good.

Young Sparks spent most of the day frowning at her grandfather. She did not approve of him getting involved in the life again, after supposedly retiring ten years previously. By her understanding, he should be in his allotment, staring down the tomato plants. In saying that, she wasn't even sure if he grew anything or if it was just a space to get out of the house for a while.

Shug and *his* grandfather, as it occurred, got on well as they worked side-by-side. Apparently, Badger had been open about the life he led and was quite happy to tell tales and teach his children and grandchildren a few things; only in private, of course. The family had been adamant that he should never discuss the business outwith familiar gatherings. However, throughout all the years, his grandfather had never mentioned his nickname. Strange.

Liam and his father had been getting along much better, too. Now that Liam knew the real story of why his father had left, all those years ago, he felt terrible about how he had treated him. The fact that Liam and his mother's safety were so important to one Cameron Buchannan that he would be willing to give up the family life he loved so much, was more than Liam could take. With that newfound knowledge, Liam found that his love for his dear old dad was beginning to return.

It was different than before, though. Liam was sixteen; no longer a child (in his own mind, at any rate). They were getting to know each other, again, but in a completely different way. Liam no longer needed someone to teach him how to ride a bicycle; or to take him to his first football match; or to tell him to get his hands out his pockets and do some work; or inform him that if he didn't finish his homework, he wasn't going out; or even build him a treehouse. He was not even able to have the honour of teaching Liam to drive.

There's still fishing, Liam thought. He had never fished properly. They had taken a couple of old rods down the river, once or twice, but they never caught any more in one day than three Kimono Micro Thin Condoms; a couple of wayward, metal frame, shopping baskets; and a long-drowned ferret.

All that being said, the two of them were doing well and beginning to feel more at home in each other's company. They were even able to smile at each other without it being forced or counterfeit. *Maybe*, Liam considered, for the first time in years, *maybe we could get back to being father and son.*

Grandads Army

That evening, upon observing Louis and the three grandfathers as they kitted themselves out with cudgel, bludgeon and cosh, Liam whispered to Sparks, 'You know, I feel like I've just joined the Home Guard. It's all a bit 'Dad's Army', isn't it.' It was not a question. When he then saw Badger take out a pistol, separate it into its individual parts and proceed to start cleaning the mechanism, *he* did start to worry. 'Are you planning on using that?' he asked the old man.

'I never expect to use it, no,' Badger replied, 'but it is better to have it and have it working than to need it and to have it jam on you. Always be prepared, that's the motto. Were you never in the Boys Brigade or the scouts?'

'Not my kind of thing,' Liam replied. 'Never seen the point in it, if I'm being honest. Just a bunch of kids, dressing up and marching off to hide out in the woods, isn't it?'

'It's a little more than that,' Badger replied. He turned to Cameron. 'You're going to have to take this boy out to the wilderness, some weekend,' he said. 'He's badly in need of an education.'

Liam's father smiled. 'I might just do that,' he replied, 'if he's up for it?'

'I suppose I could give it a go,' Liam smiled back. *Well*, he thought, *a camping trip is just as good as going fishing. Maybe we could even do both.*

Once they had determined themselves to be prepared, men, boys and girl spent some time reciting their individual objectives to each of the others as they ensured they had not missed any step. This was a big job with

351

many complex facets and it was vital that everyone did their part, perfectly.

They then selected one of the nine tactical hip packs; one strap clipped around the waist and another around the top of the thigh. Tommy had said that they were more practical for that mode of operation and would allow them quick and easy access to anything they would need, not that he thought they would need much of what they carried. Better safe than sorry was his mantra.

The Badger had placed his pistol in Cameron's safe after he had cleaned it. He now retrieved it again from the stronghold and slipped it down the back of his trousers. It was, Badger had told them, an original World War Two .455 Colt M1911, made by Colt and designed by an American named John Mosses Browning, with the metal finish and brown plastic grip.

'For goodness sake, grandad,' Shug wailed. 'Do you honestly think that down the back of your trousers is a safe place to put it?'

'Better than slipping it down the front,' Badger replied, grinning. 'I'm joking, of course. It has a safety button on the grip, Hugo. Can't fire unless you're holding on to it. Smart man that Browning.'

Liam had to admit that it *was* ingenious. He had never known that safety measures, such as this, existed; never mind all the way back in the war; longer even, if the 1911 in its name was any indication. Liam wondered, too, if the M in M1911 stood for Moses. *Probably*, he thought.

When no one had anything else to say on the matter, Tommy suggested that they get moving.

Out the back of the Ginger Nightcap, in a private and intentionally secluded carpark, there sat four, matt black, Ford Transit vans. On the side, someone had painted a picture of a lightening bold going through a house motif. Next to it were the words, 'Humphries & Younger Communications. Est. 2010'. The workmanship was professionally produced and appeared maven enough to the naked eye. If anyone saw this van parked-up on the street, they would not think too much about it.

Wishing each other the best of luck, they all entered their designated vehicles. The Grandfathers each took a van with their own grandchild. Liam, Cameron, Tommy and Louis took the final one. Their first stop would be the finish line, to drop off Liam and Tommy. Louis and Cameron would then go and pay a certain somebody a little visit, in order that they should invite him to their humble soiree.

A seven PM on the dot, the four black vans left the carpark, for their final journey, and split off in four separate directions.

All Gas and Gaiters

The ex-security guard to the Keys, Kevin Connolly, now held position at another of Ferguson's establishments, The Guid Plaice, an eatery up the east end of town. It was nowhere as upmarket as the Keys had been but it made a decent profit.

On the night in question, Kevin was stationed outside the restaurant when a black electrical van parked in Ferguson's own private space. Whether Ferguson was going to be there or not, it had been made clear to Kevin that anyone parking there should be moved on, quickly and smartly.

Kevin made his way over to the parked vehicle. It sat there, engine running. Nobody seemed to be looking to alight from it. *Maybe*, Kevin thought, *maybe they're just lost and have stopped to look at a map.*

As he reached the driver's door, he looked in through the rolled down window. Inside, he saw a small man, wearing a black boiler suit. His face was obscured by a black balaclava. The world just having come out of a two-year pandemic, Kevin understood some people's wish to remain wearing a face covering but this was a bit much. The vaccine had been rolled out a year previously and the vast majority of citizens had received their respective doses. Yet, nobody was positive if they were out of the woods or not. If some folks wished to keep their masks on, until they were more confident, then that was fine with Kevin. With some of the clientele coming in and out of Ferguson's establishments, Kevin sometimes wished that *he* was allowed to wear one, himself.

'Can I help you?' he asked the driver.

'Yes,' the driver replied, 'I'm here to see Ron, could you give him a shout for me, please. I don't want to be going inside, dressed like this. I might scare someone, eh? *Heh, Heh.*'

'Fair point,' Kevin agreed. He pulled out his radio, pressed the comm button and spoke to whoever was listening on the other end. 'I have a man in a van, out here. Says Ron's looking for him. Over.'

There was silence for a second before a reply came out. 'Okay,' the voice returned, 'he's coming out. Over and out.'

Kevin put the radio back onto his clip and looked again at the driver. 'He's on his way,' he replied. 'Can I help you with anything else before he gets here?'

'Funny you should ask that,' the mini driver answered as the side door to the back of the van slid open. There a larger gentleman crouching in the back. He was pointing a gun at the now extremely depressed security guard.

'If you would please get in the back,' the driver suggested. 'My friend will bind your hands and place a lovely velvet bag over your head. Don't be concerned. We won't hurt you.'

Kevin did as he was told and the van door slid shut.

A minute later, when Ron exited the eatery, he looked down the side of the building to where Ferguson's car usually sat. He saw the black van but Kevin, who should have been patrolling the front of the building, was absent. *I bet he's gone off for a cheeky fag*, Ron said to himself.

He walked down to where the van sat and looked through the driver's window. There was nobody to be seen. He could hear the engine running, however. 'Very strange, indeed' Ron said. This was beginning to concern him.

'Not that strange,' said a voice behind him.

Before Ron could react, he was hit, smartly on the back of the head and down he went.

Shug and Badger then loaded Ron into the back of the van. After ensuring that both their passengers were tagged and bagged, they returned to the van's cab and drove off towards their final destination.

*

The four vicenarians who had taken over Liam's mother's flat as their own, ever since Liam's presumed passing, sat as they measured out another one of their greenery shipments. When the door burst in and they were invaded by two unknowns, masked and carrying wooden battens, they found themselves well in need of a new pair of underpants. In one of their cases, this was quite literal.

'That stinks,' the smaller of the two invaders gasped.

'Just be glad you've got your mask on,' the taller one replied. 'Think how these three are going to feel, travelling in the back of the van with that mocket bastard.' He looked at the trembling boys. 'Right,' he said, pulling out four zip cords from his hip pack. 'Get your coats on. *You're coming with me.*'

The boys, in their terror, did not even think of resisting. They were so shocked and had no idea what was happening that they gave no resistance when the smaller of the two invaders tied their hands behind their backs.

When they were suitably secure, the taller one nudged the smaller. 'Which one was it that made those comments?' he asked.

The smaller one, whose long hair was trying to escape their hood, pointed at the one left of the middle.

This boy was irreverently accosted and held up against the wall by the collar. 'Listen here,' the taller one said, 'you made some indecent comments to my granddaughter. I think she deserves both an apology and some recompense.'

The boy screamed that he was sorry before bursting into tears. He hadn't signed up for this. He was even more dismayed when he was lowered to the floor again and the girl, who punched like a bear, smacked him right across the jawline. Her fist was like a brick.

'Excellent,' her grandfather applauded. 'I see you remembered what I taught you about following through with the punch. Very good.'

'Always make the first punch count,' the girl recited, smiling.

*

Angus and Baloo sat in the van, across the street from the Garland Bar and Grill.

'I'd never have guessed...' Angus began.

'Different strokes for different folks, young Aonghas,' Baloo replied. 'It's not something you can tell, just by looking at someone.'

'I know,' Angus agreed, 'but... *him*! I'd never have thought in a million years...'

'Just goes to show that you never know,' Baloo sighed.

'So,' Angus asked, 'we just sit here until he shows up?'

'Basically,' Baloo replied. 'Only, he's already in there. We're waiting for him to come out, so to speak.'

'Okay,' Angus consented. He was not keen on asking his grandfather a lot of questions. Baloo did not like that sort of thing.

Angus was in luck, however. After only thirty minutes of waiting, in complete silence, Charlie saw fit to walk out of the Garland's front door. He had company. A fresh-faced boy of around twenty years of age, followed behind him like an excited puppy.

Baloo stepped casually out of the van and ordered Angus to open the slide door. He then toddled off across the road, right towards Charlie and his new-found friend. Slipping down his mask, Baloo quick-stepped up behind the pair and wrapped his arm around Charlie's throat. Baloo held his arm in place by grabbing his wrist with the other hand. Charlie fought back at first, unsuccessfully attempting to punch Baloo in the face. His punches became slower, however, as he drifted off into unconsciousness. As his air supply was depleted, Charlie finally went still. All he heard before he went was a lilting voice, whispering, 'Hush, now. Just relax. Everything will be alright.'

Everything was not alright but there was nothing Charlie could do about it. Once Baloo had the man out cold, he lifted him up into a fireman's lift and looked, for the first time, at the speechless kid. 'You never saw a thing,' Baloo stated, 'right?'

All the boy could do was nod, fervently.

Optimistic about the boy's sincerity, Baloo turned around and carried Charlie back to the van. He tossed him into the back before joining him, inside. As he tied the man up and put the obligatory bag over his head, Angus slid the door shut and returned to the wheel. The last thing they needed when Charlie eventually woke up was him crashing around the back of the van, alerting passers-by to his kidnapping. Baloo would ensure that this did not happen.

*

When Ferguson arrived back home, that evening, he saw a black communications van pulling up behind him. When he got out and walked round his car to ask them why they were on his private property, they were already opening the back of the van. They were wearing work masks.

'Excuse me,' he said, as he strode towards them. 'What are you doing? I didn't call anyone.'

'We're here to fix the thing,' one of them replied as the other stepped into the back of the van.

'What thing?' Ferguson demanded.

'You know,' the workman continued, 'the thing that operates the.. the *thing*. You know?'

'No, I don't know,' Ferguson grunted, 'and what is your friend doing in there?'

The workman indicated that Ferguson could have a look. He did. He saw, with great surprise, if not actual fear, the second workman. He was sitting on the floor, at the opposite end of the space, pointing a shotgun at him. This did not bode well. He looked behind him, the first man had stood back a couple of feet and was now pointing another similar firearm at Ferguson's head.

'Just so's I don't have to shoot you twice,' the man replied, when questioned. 'Now, get in the back of the van, pisspot.'

367

'Wait a second,' Ferguson paused, 'don't I know you?'

The man cracked Ferguson over the head with the butt of his shotgun and watched, amiably, as Ferguson dropped to the floor, motionless.

'Quick,' the second man yelled. 'Get him in here so I can tie him up and get his bag on.'

They lifted Ferguson into the back of the van and the second man proceeded to bind his hands and feet. The first man got carefully into the driver's seat, patted his pockets as he searched for the keys and then, after finding them already in the ignition cylinder, closed the driver's door and fastened his seatbelt.

'Make it quick,' a voice echoed from behind him.

The driver nodded to himself, looked in both mirrors and pulled slowly out of the private road.

Rising Damp

Kevin and the invaders of Liam's mum's flat sat quietly, for a length of time known only to their kidnappers. All five of them were now tied to chairs. The bags remained on their heads. What room they were in or where that room was, they had no clue. All they did know was that they had been taken and trussed up without any warning. They did not know why they had been chosen to reap such terror on and were dreading the answer when it eventually arrived.

After some time, Ron came round. His head hurt and could see nothing but the internal blackness of his own bag but he was fully conscious and quite aware that he was trussed up by person or persons unknown. He said nothing, knowing there was no point, but did crack his stiff neck.

Charlie awoke soon after his colleague. When he discovered that he was tied to a chair with a bag over his head, he went nuts. Screaming obscenities at his hostage takers, he attempted to bunny-hop his chair. He was defeated in that act of derision. Some unknown person had the forethought to be there before his arrival and bolt the chair to the floor. This did not please Charlie who made a show of it. That was until a shotgun was placed under his chin. 'I suggest you take a moment to breathe,' a gruff voice advised.

This seemed to do the trick. Charlie made the lifesaving decision to keep his current opinions to himself; for the time being, at any rate.

The last to wake up was Ferguson. He, like Ron, made no fuss. He simply understood the situation and decided that he could talk himself out of it. 'I don't know who you are but you have made a big mistake. I'm a powerful man in this town. Think about that for a moment. When I get out of here, *and I will*, there will be hell to pay.'

There was silence, except for the confused Charlie. 'Boss? Is that you?'

'Do you even know who I am?' Ferguson shouted at his kidnappers. 'I'm Willie *bloody* Ferguson. I'll have your throats for this.'

'A voice, too close to his neck for comfort whispered back, 'We know who you *all* are. That's the whole fucking point.'

Ferguson's hood was whipped off at the same time as the others'. They all stared out into the room. It was badly burnt, like there had been a fire there; not too long ago, judging by the smell. The structure, however, was sound. Whoever had designed it had had the idea of lining the whole room with lead and soundproofing materials.

Therefore, the room was saved from the dreadful occurrence.

'Why have you brought us here?' Ferguson demanded.'

'This is where it all happened, another voice said.

A boy, disguised in a white masque, stepped into the room before the crescent of chairs. 'This was where I died.'

'It's you, in't it?' Ron asked.

Liam removed his mask. 'I do declare, Ronald, you are correct,' Liam answered.

'Look, I didnae ken he wuid try and kill ye,' he pleaded.

'No,' a second voice agreed, 'but you didn't do anything to stop him.'

'Fu's that?' Ron asked, screwing up his eyes in an attempt to see the man who had entered stage left.

'Well, well, well,' Ferguson laughed, 'Little Liam Macrae has found himself a playmate.

'It's not Macrae,' Liam announced.

'I'm sorry?' Ferguson asked, a little confused.

'My name isn't Macrae. That was my mother's maiden name.'

Ferguson sighed in desperation. 'So, what is your bloody name, then?' he asked. He was getting annoyed.

The new man pulled off his own mask. 'It's Buchanan,' he stated.

The look on Ferguson's face when he saw Cameron Buchanan standing before him was priceless. Then the penny dropped and he switched his gaze upon Liam.

'You're *his* kid?' he asked.

'I am,' Liam replied, 'and proud of it.'

'Look, Cammie,' he tried, 'I didn't know he was your son. If I had...'

'If you had,' Liam's father replied, 'you'd have used him to try and find me.'

Ferguson had to admit that he had a point. 'So, why have you brought us all here, then?' he inquired.

'Over the last few months, my son and his friends have had a hard time of it. They have been coerced, treated like the scum on the street and even beaten and tortured. Every one of you here tonight had a hand in that. Some more than others but a hand all the same.'

Cameron looked up and down the crescent of goons.

'Now,' Liam's father said, stepping forward into the light, 'let us see.' He walked over to the security guard and lifted his chin up with a couple of fingers. 'You held my boy down here, handcuffed for no good reason.' Tears formed and began to flow down the guards face. 'While it isn't that serious, given the circumstances of this evening, I cannot allow anyone to lay hands on my son without reprimand.' With one punch, he knocked the man out, cold. 'Take him away and drop him off outside his home. I'm done with him.'

Next in line were the four friends who had taken the proverbial piss. 'And you lot,' Liam's father growled, 'you have done your business in my home and had the nerve to think yourselves better than my own family. You are nothing but a bunch of rats and shall be treated as such. A friend of mine is going to drop you off, somewhere in the world, I've let him choose. You will be stripped down and you will be left to find your way home with no money and nothing but your underwear. I hope you put clean ones on this morning.'

They all stayed silent.

'Boy's,' Cameron continued as the boys were duly undressed by two gentlemen in gasmasks, 'I am surprised. Did you never listen to what your mothers told you? I don't know. Some people just don't take a telling.' He nodded to the gasmasks. 'Take them away.'

With that, the four boys were dragged away, off to meet their doom.

That left Ron, Charlie and Ferguson who were all remaining relatively silent.

Cameron then stepped up to Ron. 'Ron, my oldest friend. You watched as this maniac tortured my son. You knew who he was. But I also know that you did me a big favour, back in the day. So, in respect for that, I'm going to make it quick.' He pulled a pistol out from the back of his trousers. 'If you want to pray, do it now.'

Ron, knowing full well what God held in store for him, bowed his head and whispered his last words. There was a loud bang and Ron slouched down on his chair, blood dribbling from the metal studded hole that now adorned his crown.

Ferguson and Charlie looked on in shock.

'You just killed him,' Charlie wailed.

'Indeed,' Liam's father replied. 'Now, as for you... you tortured my son, not because you were ordered to, although you were, but because you enjoyed it. You are a sadistic, vile sociopath who can say or do nothing to redeem himself.' He stepped away from the frightened man, allowing Liam to step in closer.

Liam held a cosh in one hand. 'It's time you felt some of what you deal out,' Liam growled. He smacked Charlie across the face with the cosh, breaking three teeth and his jaw. Liam then dropped the cosh where he stood and took possession of a meat tenderiser, handed to him by his father. Charlie tried to scream in protest but screamed in pain, instead. His jaw slipped a little further.

The second Charlie stopped screaming, Liam brought the spiky tenderiser down on Charlie's left kneecap. They all heard the crunch. Without so much as a second's intermission, the tenderiser smashed into the right knee, too.

'Don't you think this is a bit much,' Ferguson pleaded. 'You've made your point.'

'Keep it shut,' Liam yelled. 'We'll get to you in a minute.' His face was red with anger. Liam turned back to Charlie. 'Baby gonna cry?' he asked, mocking the greeting man.

Next, Liam's father grabbed Charlie's right hand and held it flat to the arm of the chair, stretching out his fingers.

'Now,' Liam said, slowly, 'I'm not sure I can physically pull someone's fingernails out without being sick. It's just not in me to do that. So, instead...' He didn't finish his sentence. He just cracked the man's hand with the tenderiser, harder than he had his knees.'

Charlie screamed, again. The tears were flooding down his face like Niagara and onto his blood-soaked shirt by that point.

'Having fun, yet?' Liam asked. Now, what was next. Let me think. Oh, yes,' he said, as if just remembering, 'I mind, now.'

Liam's father, on cue, dropped Charlies chair so that the back was flush to the floor. Liam pulled a cloth from out of his back pocket, along with a bottle of water. He laid the cloth, with a show of great care, over Charlie's horrified countenance and leisurely poured the water over it.

Charlie squelched and spluttered and choked as he went through a virtual drowning. In the End, the water ran out and Charlie was raised back up to a seating position. He gasped for air before yelling more obscenities so vicious that they cannot be repeated.

'So,' Liam asked, 'what was it that came next? Can *you* remember?'

'Fuck you,' Charlie shouted, in defiance.

Liam spat in the man's face as a table was carried over. Atop, there was a device that Charlie recognised. 'Bring it on,' he dared. 'If you can take it, I damn well sure can.' The effort it took for him to say that much, what with having a broken jaw, was a sign of intense will.

One of the two persons who brought in the device, fiddled with it a little and passed Liam two ends, one red and one black. Liam's father then ripped Charlie's shirt open, revealing a hairy chest underneath, and poured another bottle of water all over his torso.

'Oh, dear,' Liam sighed, that's not good. This is going to hurt you a lot more than it hurt me.' He held the black alligator clip to one of Charlies water-soaked nipples, looked him dead in the eye and clamped the other one with the red.

Charlie cried out in pain. It was a long, shrill sound that only stopped when Liam lifted the first clip away. 'Now tell me,' Liam asked the weeping man, 'how did that make you feel?'

Charlie just sobbed. Liam stepped closer and whispered in his ear. 'You're not welcome around here, anymore,' he said. 'I suggest you head off somewhere remote and live a quiet life. If I ever see you again, I'll kill you, right off the bat. No questions asked. Do you understand?'

Charlie nodded, tears flooding down his face. Liam punched him hard on the face and Charlie was out for the count.

'And then there was one,' Cameron said to the room, in general.

At these words, everyone who had been coming and going, stepped up and gathered in front of Ferguson. One-by-one, they all removed their masks.

Ferguson stared at the faces before him. Apart from Cameron and Liam Buchanan, there were also Liam's three inexperienced friends; three of the previous generation's gangsters whom Ferguson had usurped many years previously; and Chief Inspector Louis Cameron. There was also one other man whom Ferguson did not recognise. He stared them all down, determined that he was not going to let them have it all their own way. 'So, what is it you're going to do with me?' he asked, calmly. 'I can't see you building up to anything worse than the torture you inflicted on one of my best men.'

'Maybe we should just stick with the torture, then,' the Badger suggested.

Baloo growled. 'Or we could skip the beginning bits and jump straight to the electrocution.'

'Now, now, gentlemen. We all settled on what was to be done with him,' Cameron reminded them. 'We all agreed that he wouldn't be hurt, so long as he gave us what we want.' He turned to face Ferguson, again and smiled.

'And what, pray, is it that you want of me?' Ferguson asked, 'Money, jewels, drink, drugs, women? Whatever you want, I'm sure we can come to an understanding.'

'I want the same thing I've been looking for, for all these years,' Cameron replied. 'The thing that stopped me from bringing up my son, in the way that I wanted.'

'And what would that be?' Ferguson asked, seeing a light at the end of this dark and bloody terrible tunnel.

Liam's father slid a small Dictaphone out from his pocket. 'I want to hear your confession,' he said.

Ferguson went stiff.

'You do know those things come in digital format, these days,' Big Grandaddy Sparks informed as Cameron checked the miniature cassette tape was fully rewound.

Cameron gave him a scolding look and ignored the well-meant suggestion. He stepped right up close to Ferguson and laid a sheet of paper on the trussed-up gangster's lap. 'Read this,' he said. 'It's your one chance to get out of here with all your bits.'

Ferguson read the sheet. 'I'm not saying this,' he informed them.

'You'd better,' Liam advised, or its jump lead time.

'No,' Ferguson replied, getting agitated. 'I have a counter-offer for you. Release me, now and I won't send every last one of my boys after you. You can leave town or you can stay and bury yourselves in the drink, I don't care, but if you don't let me go, when I do get out, and I will, you're lives won't be worth mud.'

Shug, Sparks and Angus all looked at each other as the fear started to return. What if this maniac did manage to escape, what if their plan did not work and they had to live out the rest of their years with one eye over their shoulder?

'Well, I don't think we have to worry about that,' Louis grinned. 'I had a talk with a few of my old buddies and, right now, every last one of your operations is getting raided. It's amazing what they'll do for the chance of grabbing a big fish, such as yourself. Before the morning, you won't have anything but the clothes you're sat down in.'

'They can't do that,' Ferguson bellowed. 'They need a warrant to enter any of my places and no judge is going to sign off on one with only a few words of wisdom from you, even if you did used to be a copper. That's not how things work.'

Louis grinned even more, if that were even possible. 'You see, things go a little differently when they have not one sworn testimony but five, all with no known connections to the others.'

Ferguson paused in his self-righteous rant. This had not occurred to him. 'You all gave testimony to the police?' he asked. 'You're telling me that you all turned yourselves into a lowly bunch of traitorous narks, just to get me off of the street. I'm honoured. I don't believe a word of it, though.'

'Believe it,' Cameron said. 'We all wrote them down, signed them, sealed them and Louis here delivered them. All nice and legal.'

'We even went so far as to sign our real names,' Baloo added. 'Not often I let the man have my details but I'm willing to risk the wrath of big brother, if it gets you out of the picture.'

Ferguson was stunned. He sat there for a minute as he eyed them all up and down, assessing whether or not he believed them. Their faces were nothing but stern and honest. He came to a decision.

Absolutely Fabulous

It was a bright sunny morning when the police arrived to take Ferguson away. They listened to the tape, unable to contain their delight. After that, it was time for the enraged confessor to be escorted down to the station for a face-to-face with the boys and girls in the Major Crimes division. There would be a party in the Blue and Two, that evening and no mistake.

Ferguson had made a show of consternation but, with so many signed statements and an actual confession tape, he was banged to rights. There would be a raid at his home and all his businesses. The local constabulary had been itching to do this for many years and now, thanks to Liam, his father and the rest of the crew, it was Christmas, Easter and every other public holiday rolled into one. They had fought for so long to get even a peep inside Ferguson's business but without any hard evidence, no judge was about to write them a script. Any warrant given would have to be based on something concrete; and I am not talking wellies, here.

But it was done and dusted. They had their evidence and before the lunch bell rang throughout the town, they would have their warrant. Ferguson was screwed and there was nothing he or his lawyers could do about it.

Liam was sure that he would claim that the tape was recorded under duress but with not a single mark on him, there was not a jury in the world that would choose to believe him. Ferguson was too well known and any jury would be sure to have a majority who, not to put too strong a point on it, disliked the man considerably. Many people had come to discover what Ferguson was truly like and a great many of them knew at least one other who had been brought low because of him.

To put it bluntly, Ferguson was not a popular man and he would have a hard time convincing anyone in Kilmarnock or the surrounding area that he was being set up. Ferguson's solicitor would still try and argue the gangster's case but even she would know that he was going down. Liam was positive that she would be presenting Ferguson with an invoice of some considerable worth which he would be wise to pay before the closing arguments.

Liam, on the other hand, was just relieved that their ordeal was finally over. The cleaner had been called in to dispose of Ron's body and remove any and all evidence that they had been there, let alone having committed all number of offences. Liam was amazed. This sort of thing usually only happened in the movies. It had never occurred to him that the movies had not invented such things but, instead, had borrowed them from real life characters.

Liam and the others left the cleaner to the business which she knew best. Then they all, unilaterally, decided that what they needed at that exact point was to head back to the Ginger Nightcap for, well, a *golden nightcap*. Just this once, Liam's father allowed him one single measured nip of the water of life. He had enjoyed a little more than that when his father was not looking but with Ferguson out of the picture, Cameron Buchanan was able to be a dad to his son, once again, and all that that entailed.

They had agreed that Liam's mother's flat would be put up for sale and the profits, alongside a little extra which his father would add to the pot, would be used to buy a nicer place where the boy could live without any unfortunate memories getting in the way. Liam's father had bought the flat off of the council may years before he had retired from Ferguson's business and it had served them well. Every bill had been paid on time and all work that required attention had been delt with quickly and with no shortcuts. The flat, therefore, was the best kept home on the estate. They would certainly get above the odds for it.

For that night, though, Liam would sleep under the roof of the Ginger Nightcap. After the summer, Liam's father insisted, his son and heir would return to school for his final year. He would have a word with the headmaster who had written Liam off of the books when he didn't show up for six months in a row. Liam's father was sure that he would be able to explain matters to the man in such a way that would ensure

Liam's return. After that, it would be Liam's choice of whether he wanted to attend university or work alongside Cameron.

Liam had been brought up to date with what his father referred to as *the family business*. Cameron had set up a sort of secret society, called the Honourable Brothers of the Provincial Tribunal. It was their objective to proceed where the official authorities were not able to go and do that which they were not allowed to do. The Brotherhood, as they were known, would receive information from the general public and police alike. Anyone who thought themselves to be beyond the law would discover that they were gravely mistaken. Thieves who thought they got away with it; drug dealers who sold to kids; and murderers who were too clever for their own good would all be taken down a peg and delt with accordingly. Occasionally, certainly with the murderers, there would be more than just a handover to the police. If no evidence was found that the police could use to convict then some other arrangements would be decided on by the tribunal and steps would be taken to ensure that sort of thing never happened again.

'So, you're a real-live Batman, then?' Liam had asked.

'If that's how you want to look at it,' his father replied.

'Just like last night?' Liam asked.

'Not usually, no,' his father rebuffed. 'Usually, we deal with situations that are a lot less complicated. Ferguson was a special case.'

Liam smiled at this. He was not sure that he would be able to keep up the pace if every job went the way it had done on the previous night. It had all been a bit too much for him. He was sure the other three felt the same.

As he looked around the bar, he could see Shug and young Sparks cosied up in a booth, sound asleep. Angus was lying on the pool table, through the house. It was anyone's guess when he would rouse again. *Still*, Liam thought, *it is probably the best sleep he's had in a long time. Certainly, the first he has gotten without getting stoned, first.*

All-in-all, everyone was enjoying the rest, the peace and the quiet while they could. It had been a busy time for them all, especially the young ones, and it was nice to be able to stop and not worry about whether they were going to be dead by the end of the day. With Ferguson, Ron and Charlie out of the picture for good, none of them had a care in the world. Happiness flowed like a good whisky and they were going to make the best of it.

Bless This House

The next day, Liam went back to his mother's old flat. The place was a mess and it took him, Shug, Sparks and even Angus a good six hours to gather up all the weed, accoutrements and rubbish which the invaders had left behind. When they had done this, they weighed up the weed, just to see what was there. When they had counted as much as ten kilos and still had more than half to go, they gave up. It was clear that they would have enough for their own personal use to last them a good long time; longer now that Angus had been forcibly put on his grandfather's one step program. Angus, whether from respect or fear, would never touch a spiff again.

Liam said goodbye to his mother's flat with a good long smoke from the strongest smelling bag they had. He spent the night, lying on his couch, remembering his dear mother and the good old days before he was sucked into the bloody business that he had been. It had undeniably happened, though, there was no denying it and now it was done. Whether or not he would join his father in the family business, a year or three later, he was still unsure. Right now, all his thoughts were fond memories of his mother and how much he had loved her.

Porridge

Ferguson sat in his six-by-eight prison cell, his bunkmate, above him, snoring like he had a trombone stuck up one nostril. It was less than ideal but he would do something about it in the morning.

He was furious. This was understandable but his rage grew inside him until he passed through being manic, to finding a place of relative peace. He took all the anger and frustration and rolled it up into one big ball of determination. He resolved, quite quickly after entering H.M.P. Kilmarnock, more commonly named Bowhouse Prison, that he would get retribution for what had been done to him. He remembered every face that had been there, that night. Each and every one of them would pay for their part in his demise.

Ferguson, unbeknown to most, still had one friend in this world. He had sent them a message via one of the more financially strapped guards and was expecting news very soon.

There was a rap on the cell door and a piece of paper, sealed, was slipped through the small hole in the door. Ferguson rolled off of his bunk and collected the paper from where it had landed. He read it. He smiled.

Distracted by the sudden trumpet call from his bunkmate's derailed sinuses, Ferguson looked up from his news and decided that he could take some time to rectify the man's adenoidal functions, after all. Whether or not the man would be able to breathe at all after Ferguson played doctor was another matter. Carefully and making sure not to arouse the snorer, Ferguson walked over to the small sink. Retrieving the snorer's own toothbrush,

Ferguson lined it up to the offending nostril before ramming it straight up, hammering it in with the back of his fist. Before the snorer could complain, his eyes opened wide, crossed and he drifted away.

That night, Ferguson slept the sleep of Angels without a single sound from above. The guards would find him in the morning but that was hours away. Ferguson felt sure he could convince them it was a suicide; making Ferguson angry, usually was.